A Cotswold Christmas

A Cotswold Christmas

A Willoughby Close Romance

KATE HEWITT

TULE
PUBLISHING

Chapter One

"I'M SO SORRY. I did send you an email..." Frances Heath's forehead crinkled with concern as she trailed off apologetically.

Anna Vere tried for a valiant smile, the determinedly lifted chin. She felt like stamping her foot and shrieking. Or worse, bursting into tears. "It's... fine."

But was it fine? The bed & breakfast where she'd booked her Christmas holiday, in this picturesque chocolate-box-worthy village in the English Cotswolds, was flooded. Or rather, her bedroom on the ground floor was flooded. The carpet had squelched under their feet as Frances had shown her the dire state of the room, the smell of encroaching mildew in the air, pointing out the damp on the walls and the water pooling in the corners as if she was afraid Anna might think she was lying.

"I tried to find alternative accommodation for you," Frances continued, her arthritic hands pleating together anxiously, "but it's December twenty-second. Absolutely everything is booked, you know. People love coming to the

Cotswolds for the holidays."

"Of course," Anna murmured.

She stood there staring, barely able to take in the disastrous turn her holiday had taken. She'd flown in from New York that morning, she hadn't slept in eighteen hours, and now she no place to stay. Christmas was officially ruined, but it had pretty much been ruined already. A Travel Lodge on the M6 wasn't really going to change all that much.

"Cup of tea?" Frances asked with hopeful brightness, and Anna murmured a thank-you. Why not? A cup of tea was a Brit's answer to almost everything. Too bad it wasn't big enough to sleep in.

She followed Frances back to the front room of the tumbledown cottage of golden Cotswold stone that she'd found on the Internet. It had looked perfect, chintzy and comfortable without being romantic. She definitely didn't need romantic. Now a Christmas tree perched precariously in one corner and a manger scene took pride of place on the deep windowsill, its bowed glass overlooking the village green, dusk settling over it peacefully.

Frances led her to the kitchen in the back of the house, where a kettle was already hissing cheerfully on top of a bright red, Aga cooking range, along with a rack of freshly baked shortbread decorated with red and green sprinkles. A gray cat sat on the windowsill, its tail swishing back and forth, looking regal and suspicious as only cats could.

The simple comfort of the scene made jet lag sweep over

Anna, causing her shoulders to slump and stupid tears to sting her eyes. Where on earth was she going to sleep tonight, never mind the rest of the two-week vacation she'd booked? She didn't feel strong or stable enough to face this problem.

"So I wasn't able to find similar bed and breakfast accommodation," Frances said as she bustled about making tea, speaking in a brisk way as if this wasn't the enormous problem it felt to Anna. "But then I had a sudden idea. My cousin is just finishing renovating some lovely cottages in the next village, Wychwood-on-Lea. Willoughby Close, they're called. He renovated the stables of the big manor house there and they're going to be let in the new year, but they're empty now. So I thought, why not have you stay there?"

She handed Anna a cup of tea that she accepted with thanks, grateful for the warmth that seeped into her cradled palms. The bus-to-train-to-cab journey from Heathrow had been full of traffic and sleeting rain. Not exactly the magical, snowy Christmas she'd been hoping for, but this was England, after all. Rain was the norm.

"You mean"—Anna clarified—"you have somewhere for me to stay?"

"Well, yes, if you don't mind being in a different village. Wychwood-on-Lea is lovely, though, right on the river. And the cottages are beautiful, lots of period details. Colin showed me..." Frances trailed off, as she seemed to have a habit of doing, and took a sip of tea.

"That sounds wonderful." At this point she didn't have the energy to be picky, as long as there was a bed and a roof. And preferably heating. "How do I get there?"

Frances pursed her lips. "I'll ask Colin to come here and pick you up."

"I don't want to put him out of his way…" And she didn't want to make laborious chitchat with a complete stranger, not when she was jet-lagged and exhausted. Not when she'd come to England so she could curl up by herself, lick her wounds, and hopefully heal.

"It's no trouble." Frances assured her. "Colin's always happy to help. I'll ring him now and he should be here in twenty minutes." Frances bustled off before Anna could say another thank-you.

She sat back and sipped her tea, closing her eyes as she fought another wave of fatigue. Bed. She really just wanted her bed, or any bed. A pillow, a mattress, and a duvet, a good twelve hours of sleep. That didn't seem like too much to ask.

"Yes, Colin is coming right now," Frances said in a tone of almost maternal satisfaction as she came back into the kitchen. "I'm sure you'll be very comfortable at Willoughby Close."

"Thank you," Anna said "You're very kind."

"I'm sorry this happened at all," Frances clucked. "And at Christmas, too." She cocked her head, her bright, inquisitive eyes reminding Anna of a sparrow. "You've come a long way, then?"

"From New York City."

"Ah, lovely. I always wanted to visit. See that Times Square everyone goes on about. Is it as exciting as they say?" Anna opened her mouth to answer but Frances rattled on before she managed a syllable. "But you've come on your own, dear? For Christmas?"

Anna steeled herself against the note of pity in the older woman's voice. Christmas by oneself generally sounded a bit pathetic, but it was what she wanted. Needed, even. She couldn't face the family Christmas, her parents bustling around anxiously. Not this year, and staying cooped up in her apartment in New York while everyone else went home for the holiday or made bright party plans was too depressing for words. She wanted to get away, at least for a little while. Too bad she couldn't get away from herself.

"Yes, I've been working a lot recently and wanted the break," she said, injecting a note of finality into her voice. *Please don't ask any more questions.*

"Oh, of course. A change is as good as a rest, they say." Frances nodded, not looking convinced by her own statement.

Anna took another sip of tea, relief pulsing through her when the she heard a man's voice coming from the front hallway. Her lift, she hoped, was here.

"Frances…"

"Oh, it's Colin." Frances brightened. "In the kitchen, Colin!"

Seconds later a man appeared in the doorway, seeming to take up all the space and making Anna blink. He wasn't what she'd been expecting, which was the male version of Frances—well into his sixties, with an affable, chatty manner, a shock of white hair, and lots of wrinkles. Colin Heath didn't have any of those things.

He was built like a rugby player, big and muscular, his shoulders nearly spanning the doorframe, his movements easy yet powerful. He wore an old flannel shirt and faded jeans stuck into battered work boots, and his eyes were a light, startling blue in a face tanned by working outdoors, Anna suspected, rather than sitting in the sun. Short, light brown hair stuck up as if he'd thoughtlessly raked his fingers through it. He couldn't be much more than Anna's own thirty-five.

His blue eyes fastened on hers and his mouth turned up in a friendly, easy smile; two dimples appeared in his craggy cheeks. "You must be Anna."

It disconcerted her that he knew who she was, which was silly since Frances had probably explained everything on the telephone. "Yes." For some reason Anna felt herself going all stiff and overly polite. She gave him a quick little smile and then covered her unease by sipping more tea.

"Sorry to hear about the flooding." Anna couldn't tell whether he was addressing her or Frances. "Not the best way to spend Christmas, eh?"

She murmured a bland agreement. She didn't really want

to talk about Christmas. Perhaps she should have booked a hotel in London, somewhere sleek and anonymous, where no one would attempt to get to know her. But she'd wanted to escape city life, hole up somewhere cozy and quaint, go for long, snowy walks through the hills—or wolds, considering this was the Cotswolds, a gentle land of rolling hills and movie-set-worthy villages between Oxford and Bath. And there was no snow to be seen.

"Well, at least you'll have a roof over your head," Colin said cheerfully. "Although not much more than that."

Wait—what? Anna stared at him uncertainly.

"Don't worry." He assured her. "I've got some kit."

Kit? What was that? This was sounding more and more alarming. And yet somehow the words out of her mouth were, "I'm sure it will be fine." When had she become such a pushover? When she'd become too tired to fight, which had been about three months ago.

"Shall we get going, if you've finished your cuppa? It's getting dark."

"Of course." Anna rose from her seat as Frances fluttered about her.

"I'm *so* sorry," she said as she wrung her hands. "I'll give you a full refund, of course..."

You certainly will. Anna thought sourly. She was starting to feel seriously grumpy. Still she managed to say, "Don't worry. All I need is a place to stay."

"Good thing." Colin chipped in, and Anna shot him another uncertain look. What was Willoughby Close, exactly?

He easily hoisted her suitcase as she followed him out to the battered Land Rover parked in the narrow lane in front of Meadow Cottage. Colin tossed her bag in the back and then opened the passenger side door.

"Sorry, it's a bit of a tip. I'm not the neatest bloke."

No, he was not. Anna eyed the sea of paper coffee cups, crumpled napkins and maps, and a browning banana peel on the floor of the Rover. She wasn't all that squeamish, but she was wearing nice boots. Nudging the banana peel aside with the toe of her designer leather boot, she clambered inside.

"So what brought you across the pond for Christmas?" Colin asked as he started down the lane, his wing mirrors nearly clipping the dry stone walls on either side of the road, although he didn't so much as blink.

"I just felt like getting away." Which was his cue not to ask any more questions.

In case he didn't get the message, Anna turned to look out the window at the ivy-covered cottages streaming by. The rain had stopped and the sky was awash in lavender; a Christmas tree had been set up in the middle of the green, strung with multi-colored lights.

Through the oncoming dusk, Anna saw a mother pushing a baby carriage, smiling down into its quilted depths. She looked away quickly, focusing instead on the pub across the street and its promise of mulled wine and mince pies every evening from now until New Year's. She hoped Wychwood-on-Lea had a pub.

Fortunately Colin didn't ask any more questions, at least not until he'd driven down several narrow, winding roads lined by dry stone walls with fields and meadows rolling to the horizon on either side, and then into a village whose sign announced it was Wychwood-on-Lea and runner-up of Britain in Bloom for 2007.

"So where exactly am I staying?" Anna asked as Colin drove down the village's high street, a quaint, narrow lane with a few shuttered shops, a church, and at its end a village green that had a semi-dilapidated play park, an impressive war memorial, and another lit-up Christmas tree.

"Willoughby Close. Willoughby Manor is just outside the village. They converted the stables to a set of four cottages. I did the renovation work."

Which was what Frances had told her, but Anna didn't really feel like she had any more information about her actual accommodation. "But they're empty now?"

"No one's moving in until the new year."

"How come? I mean, I would have thought there would be some interest in renting over Christmas."

"Oh, they're not holiday lets," Colin said as he made a sharp left through some intricate, wrought iron gates. In the distance Anna saw the peaked gables of an Elizabethan manor house silhouetted against the darkening sky. "They're long-term lets. The first tenant is moving in on January first."

"Right…" She paused, her jet-lagged brain clicking gears a little slowly. "But they're furnished?" Her voice wobbled as she spoke, unsure if she was stating the ridiculously obvious.

"Furnished?" Light brown eyebrows drew together over his piercingly blue eyes. "No, ah, not exactly."

Anna tensed. "What does that mean?"

"Not at all, actually." He had the grace to look slightly abashed. "I gather Frances didn't tell you the details?"

Anna couldn't keep the acid from her voice as she answered, "Frances told me I would be quite comfortable."

"Ah." He'd swung into a sweeping drive, bypassing the curving graveled lane that led to the manor house to jolt over a dirt track that was more potholes than not. "She was being a bit optimistic, I think."

"Really." Anna couldn't keep herself from resorting to a little soft sarcasm. She was extremely tired, not to mention emotionally more than a little bit fragile. Together it was not a good combination.

He glanced at her, frowning. "Sorry, this isn't exactly the holiday you envisioned, is it? I mean, obviously…"

Anna felt a lump form in her throat, ridiculously big. She turned to the window to hide how close to tears she'd suddenly become.

The last thing she needed was to fall apart in front of a stranger. "No."

"I did bring some of my camping kit. A sleeping bag, some pots and pans. The cooking range works…"

Dear heaven. It was worse than she'd thought. "Why don't you show me the place?" She managed to speak through a too-tight throat.

Colin stopped the Land Rover in a little cobbled court-yard, the former stables framing it on three sides. From the outside, the cottages looked pretty, low buildings of golden Cotswold stone with peaked roofs and mullioned windows, flower pots, empty in winter, by the doors. "Number one is the most finished," he said and Anna turned to him with a start.

"What do you mean, the *most* finished?"

"The upstairs bath needs a final bit of tiling work. I was going to do it after Christmas." He got out of the car and Anna did the same, dread seeping into her stomach. How was she going to spend two weeks in an entirely empty house? Well, she wouldn't. She'd stay the night and then figure something else out in the morning. There had to a hotel room going spare even on December twenty-third, in one of the quaintest parts of England.

Colin unlocked the door, stepping aside so Anna could enter first. Taking a deep breath, she did. The house was entirely dark, so the smell hit her first—fresh paint and plaster, overlaid by that funny scent of new appliances or cars—it was, she realized as she stood there blinking in the dark, a lonely smell. An empty smell. Maybe if she'd been in a different frame of mind she could have considered this funny or even exciting, a new start, an adventure. As it was, she was starting to feel like she'd swallowed a bowling ball and now had to drag it around in her stomach.

"So." Colin flicked on the lights and Anna blinked in the sudden brightness, taking in an open plan kitchen and living area. It looked bright and airy, with a woodstove and French doors that led to a little terrace out back. The appliances were gleaming, the counters spotless. It was completely empty.

"Well, then," Colin said, and his voice echoed through the empty rooms, bouncing off bare walls and stone-tiled floors. "Welcome to Willoughby Cottage."

Chapter Two

C OLIN FELT A stab of pity for the woman who stood next to him, her face pale and her dark blue eyes wide as she took in the empty cottage. Clearly she wasn't about to appreciate his plastering work.

"If we get a fire going, things might start to look cozy," he said with a lot more optimism than he felt.

His cousin was the most muddleheaded woman he'd ever met. Why on earth had she thought a guest expecting a double bed, a private bathroom, fresh towels and clean sheets, not to mention a decent fry-up every morning, would be remotely comfortable in a cold, empty house? He'd only turned the electricity on that afternoon. But that was Frances, optimistic to the point of blindness. Goodness only knew how she'd managed to keep the B&B running all this time.

"I think it would take more than a fire to make things feel cozy," Anna said. Her lips trembled and she pressed them together. "Though it seems like a very nice cottage. I'm sure it will be fabulous when it's furnished."

"Right." He watched her for a moment, noting the dark circles under her eyes, the way her pale, flawless skin seemed stretched tightly over her cheekbones. She looked exhausted, which was understandable, but more than that she looked sad. An air of sorrow, of deep and intense sadness, hung about her like a cloud, followed her like a dark shadow. He didn't think he'd ever met someone whose emotions emanated from them like a sonar pulse. He didn't like the thought of her slumming it in here by herself, but what else could he do? He doubted there was an empty hotel room from here to Edinburgh.

"Let me get some firewood," he said, and brushed by her to go outside. He loaded up on firewood from the shed by the side of the house and then came back inside, busying himself with building a fire in the little woodstove.

Anna wandered around the room, her arms wrapped around herself, her long hair streaming down her back in a dark ribbon. Colin's gaze wandered towards her slim figure encased in an expensive-looking cashmere sweater and skinny jeans, knee-high leather boots emphasizing her slender calves. She looked like she had money, but that wouldn't help her if there weren't any rooms available.

"I could call some places, if you like," he said.

This woman wasn't his problem but he couldn't keep from feeling at least partially responsible. When Frances had called him, blathering about flooding and the cottages, Colin had envisioned an entirely different scenario. An entirely different person, someone who wasn't bothered by details and just needed a place to kip for a night or two. Not a paying guest who had been intending on having a proper holiday, who looked like she'd never roughed it in her life. Considering Frances' history of muddling things up, he supposed he should have been more suspicious.

Anna turned to look at him, her ink-dark hair flying about her shoulders. "I thought you said everything would be booked."

"It most likely is," Colin agreed as he straightened. A cheerful blaze emanated from the little woodstove, and he couldn't decide if it made the place cozier or more depressing, the dancing shadows highlighting the complete barrenness of the room. "But I could try."

"It's already dinnertime," Anna replied with a shrug. "I can sleep here for a night and figure things out in the morning."

"I can give you a list of local places…"

"Thank you." She pressed her lips together; the shadows under her eyes were as dark as bruises. "You said you had some… kit?"

"Oh, right. I'll get it now." Colin headed back outside; it was now completely dark, the blackness that settled over the rolling countryside unrelieved by a single streetlight. Willoughby Manor was on the edge of Wychwood-on-Lea, but it might as well have been in the deepest, darkest countryside. The unease he'd felt since setting eyes on Anna Vere settled more deeply in his gut, his very bones. He couldn't leave this fragile-looking woman on her own in an empty cottage near Christmas. He didn't think of himself as a boy scout, although he always tried to help a neighbor. But Anna Vere's air of quiet desperation spoke to him. Touched him, somehow.

He grabbed the sleeping bag and box of camping kit and headed back inside. She was standing by the French windows, gazing out at the darkened garden, her back to him. Colin set the box of kit down on the kitchen counter with a clank. He realized he hadn't brought a pillow or sleeping mat, or a towel for that matter.

"Look, I'm afraid I didn't realize what the situation was here," he said, and cleared his throat, feeling unusually awkward.

He liked feeling helpful, capable. He was used to it, but there was something about Anna's sense of containment, her stillness and silence, that made him feel like a clumsy giant, all thick fingers and brick-like feet.

"When Frances got me on the phone, she was rattling on about flooding and the like... I don't know, I didn't twig that she was talking about a guest who had booked in for a while, for a proper holiday." At least not a guest like Anna, whose expensive clothes and air of fragility did not bode well for roughing it in an empty house. He shook his head ruefully. "I don't know what I thought. But I would have... well, I would have brought more kit, for starters."

Anna turned to him with a small, tired smile. "I'm sure I can manage for one night with what you've brought. You're very kind."

"Yes," Colin continued doggedly, "but why should you have to? I only live a few minutes away. I'll go back and grab a few extra bits—a pillow and towel, at least. You'll want a bath."

Her eyebrows rose teasingly. "I thought the bath wasn't finished?"

"I just need to finish the tile round the sink. But the bath is done, and it's a lovely one. Big, claw-footed beast, perfect for having a soak." And then, maybe because he was a man or simply because Anna was an undoubtedly beautiful woman, he pictured her lounging in the tub, her dark hair flowing over her shoulders, a few strategic bubbles hiding the best bits and then popping slowly...

Colin felt a flush rising to his face and he turned away quickly, embarrassed by his own thoughts. He really wasn't that kind of sad tosser. At least, he hoped he wasn't.

"Anyway, it's no trouble. Won't take a minute."

"Well... if you're sure..." Anna didn't sound sure, but then the whole situation must seem surreal to her. Camping in an empty house instead of the cozy B&B she'd been planning.

"I'm sure," Colin said firmly, and as he glanced at Anna he was treated to her first proper smile. It lit up her face, her eyes glowing like blue stars, transforming the air of sadness into something else entirely. For a few seconds Colin felt like he'd been tasered.

"Thank you," she said. "That really is very kind."

"Um. Yeah. Right." He blinked, coming back into himself as Anna's smile faded. He couldn't remember when a woman had affected him so much. Her smile had felt like a spotlight being swung on him, leaving him blinking in its brilliance. "Be back in a couple of ticks," he said, and then hurried out without looking at her again.

AFTER THE DOOR closed Anna wandered around the downstairs, feeling fuzzy-headed from fatigue and yet weirdly hopeful, too. After that first awful realization when she'd seen the cottage looking so depressingly empty, things had, for no apparent reason, started to feel better. It was only for one night, and there was sure to be some kind of hotel room available somewhere in all of England. Tomorrow she could be living in luxury; maybe she'd treat herself, try for something truly five-star, a king-sized bed and a whirlpool bath, spa treatments, and continuous room service.

But it wasn't her own halfhearted talking-to that had cheered her up; it was Colin's presence. There was something so capable and reassuring about him, the way he'd taken charge without having to think about it. She'd been weirdly mesmerized by his strong hands as he'd loaded wood into the stove, the way his worn jeans strained across his thighs as he'd crouched in front of it. He was good-looking in a rough-hewn way, with his craggy face and powerful body, so different from Mark's city polish and smooth urbanity, all slick hair and tailored suits. There was something honest and open about Colin, something real, that Anna instinctively liked and trusted.

Stupid to think that way about a stranger, of course, but she was feeling vulnerable and alone and a little kindness went an embarrassingly long way. Still, he'd drop off a few more supplies and then she'd probably never see him again. She'd be out of here in the morning, off to who-knew-where.

Sensing her spirits were about to start plummeting again, Anna decided to investigate the upstairs. A steep, narrow staircase led from the front hall to a landing with two bedrooms and a bathroom leading off. Original blackened beams ran along the freshly-plastered ceilings. The bedrooms were small but well-fitted, with built-in wardrobes and lovely big windows. The bathtub was just as Colin had promised— free-standing and claw-footed, deep and long, perfect for a lovely, long soak. Anna was tempted to have one later; tension knotted her neck and shoulder blades.

From the bathroom window she looked out at rolling fields lit up only by a sliver of moon, the manor house visible in the distance, no more than a peaked roof above the stark tree line. It was a peaceful, pretty place, even on a winter evening; she could imagine taking walks out in those fields, coming in after to curl up by the wood stove with a cup of tea…

If only there was furniture. And dishes. And sheets. Sighing, she turned from the window. Tomorrow she would get on the phone and figure out a place to stay for the next two weeks. Surely there had to be something.

About twenty minutes later the sound of wheels on gravel had Anna sighing with relief. Yes, this spot was peaceful, but there was something fairly unnerving about being alone in an empty house in the middle of nowhere, when she was practically swaying from tiredness.

"I'm back," Colin announced unnecessarily as he came into the living area, bringing in a blast of cold, fresh air and a whiff of some kind of aftershave—cedar, maybe, or pine. "Brought a few things, as well as some dinner. I realized you most likely haven't eaten."

"I haven't," Anna admitted, although she wasn't all that hungry. Her stomach was five hours behind, along with the rest of her body. "Thank you."

"So." Colin heaved a big cardboard box on top of the counter. "Pillow, check. Towel, check. Teabags. Some milk and cereal and bread for the morning, and a few extra comforts." He waved a large bar of luxury dark chocolate. "It is Christmas, after all."

"You're too kind," Anna said, ridiculously touched by his effort. "I can reimburse you—"

"Nonsense." Colin waved aside her token offer. "Frances got you into this mess. This is the least I can do."

"Frances did, not you." Anna pointed out. "You're what? Her cousin?"

"Second cousin once removed, actually, but my family has always been close."

"That sounds nice."

"Sometimes. Sometimes it makes me contemplate murder. I have three older, very nosy, very bossy sisters."

"Oh, dear. That sounds… challenging."

"That's one way of putting it."

Anna watched Colin move about, putting food in the fridge and then taking a stack of paper plates out of the box. "Sorry, let me help. I'm just standing here watching you…"

"It's fine." Once again he waved away her offer. "You must be exhausted. You took an overnight flight?"

"A late overnight flight. The plane was delayed and we didn't leave until one in the morning. It took all day to clear customs and get myself out here."

"Only to find you were homeless. That is tough luck."

"It could happen to anybody, I suppose."

"Still. Not a great way to spend Christmas." He was easing off the foil lids of two containers and the smell of spicy curry wafted out, stirring Anna's appetite. "I hope you like tikka masala? Britain's national dish."

"Love it," Anna said.

She'd always liked a simple curry or burger; Mark had been the one to prefer Michelin stars and tiny, gourmet portions artfully arranged on hexagonal plates.

"Good." Colin looked up, his blue eyes meeting hers as he grinned, and Anna smiled back, strangely jolted by the look in his eyes, the sense of complicity and connection. This was almost starting to feel like some bizarre date, and no more so when then Colin drew a bottle of wine out of the box.

"Fancy a glass…?" he asked, and then paused, a frown marring his features before a surprising blush rose in his cheeks. "Oh no, does this all seem terribly creepy to you? A strange bloke comes in bearing wine and takeaway… honestly, it's not like that." His face was fiery now, and so was Anna's.

"No, it's not creepy at all," she said quickly, because it wasn't, not remotely, and yet she *had* been thinking along date-like lines. Stupidly. "You're being so incredibly kind. I really am thankful."

"Okay." He put the bottle on the counter with a clunk. "We don't have to have the wine." His face was still red, and Anna found it strangely endearing.

"Actually, I'd love a glass of wine." Why not? It was nearly Christmas, after all, and she needed to find her pleasures where she could. "Thank you."

Colin looked a little relieved as he opened the bottle and poured two plastic tumblers full. "Well, cheers then," he said as he handed her a glass. "Here's to Christmas getting a whole lot better for you."

"It can only go up from here, can't it?" Anna answered

lightly, and took a sip. The wine was surprisingly good. She wondered where Colin had got it from. His own supply? He was really being incredibly generous.

Colin brought their food towards the wood stove, and they sat on the floor in front of it, plates balanced on their laps, the fire casting flickering shadows over their faces as they ate.

"So what made you decide to come to this corner of the world for Christmas?" Colin asked.

He ate the way Anna would have expected, with lots of relish and big bites, clearly enjoying his food. She liked it somehow, so different from Mark's prissy, precise little bites. He'd always cut his asparagus into equal lengths, a fact that annoyed Anna in retrospect. But why was did she keep comparing Colin to Mark? She barely knew this man. And yet what she knew, she liked.

"I wanted to get away for a bit," she answered his question, toying with a few grain of rice on the tines of her fork. "Life had all become a bit... much." Which made it sound as if she'd been halfway to having a nervous breakdown, and maybe she had, but... she didn't really want Colin thinking that about her.

"Understandable, but it's still quite a drastic move on your own, isn't it? Do you know anyone out here?"

"No." She forced a smile. "I suppose it seems pathetic, going away on my own for Christmas, but I wanted some quiet and space to think through things." Colin frowned and

Anna continued in a rush, "I've recently broken it off with my fiancé. Well, he broke it off, but it was heading that way for a while. I wanted some time to take stock, figure out what to do next."

"I'm sorry." He looked both uncomfortable and appalled. "I'm being horrendously nosy, aren't I, badgering you like this? Just tell me to stop."

"Okay," Anna answered, smiling. "Stop."

Colin grinned, his face creasing in a way that was already starting to feel familiar. "Well, that's me told. But why the Cotswolds? It's a pretty place, of course, but most Americans choose London." He raised his eyebrows. "Is that too personal a question? You can tell me to shut up again, really."

"No, it's fine," Anna said with a little laugh. "I live in New York City, and I didn't feel like going to another big city. I went on vacation in this area once, with my parents, when I was about sixteen. I thought it would be nice to come back." And she hadn't wanted to face Christmas with her mom and dad, who would have been fussing over her every second, wondering if she was okay, asking anxiously if she wanted to *talk*. She didn't, not about Mark, and definitely not about the other stuff. She could barely cope with thinking about that yet. She'd tried not to think about it for the last three months, and yet it hovered on the edge of her brain, a black spot in her peripheral vision, ever looming closer.

"Well, hopefully we can find a place for you to stay that's not too far away." He sounded doubtful.

"Maybe I'll just stay here." Colin looked as surprised as Anna felt. Where had that come from? "You've kitted me out pretty well, haven't you?" she continued, feeling a little reckless now, a bit giddy. She'd only had a few sips of wine. "It looks like a lovely spot, and I had a peek at that bath. Five-star accommodation right there."

Colin's mouth curved. "I am proud of that bath. Fitted it myself."

"It's all lovely, really." She looked around the room, imagining it with a couple of squashy sofas, an oak table and chairs. Country furniture, comfortable and classic, a little beaten up. Not like the chrome and glass monstrosities Mark preferred. *Stop thinking about Mark.* "You said it's been rented?"

"Yes, a single mum and her daughter. They came and looked at it last week. They're moving here from up north in the new year."

"And what about the other cottages?"

"Not yet, but I think they'll go fast. Like you said, it's a nice spot, and you can walk into the village."

"Can you? Are there shops there? Will I be able to manage without a car?"

"You're serious about staying?" Colin said. He sounded surprised.

Anna shrugged. "Why not? It beats calling a hundred

hotels only to be told there's no room at the inn." She gave him a whimsical smile. "Very appropriate, in a way, considering the season."

"Indeed." Colin was chewing slowly, seeming lost in thought. Anna's breath hitched. Was she crazy, to think she could stay here for two whole weeks, roughing it in a sleeping bag, with a single towel? "There's a post office shop in the village," he said after a moment. "And a couple of pubs and takeaway places. You should manage all right. But if you like, you could have dinner with my family tomorrow night. It's a bit of a brawl but you're more than welcome."

"Oh." Anna tried to rearrange her expression into something pleased and polite. His *family*. Why hadn't she considered that? Of course he was married with a couple of kids. He seemed like the kind of guy who would be—relaxed, comfortable in his own skin. She could picture a toddler perched on his shoulder, a baby braced easily in the crook of one large arm. The image sent pain slicing through her and she quickly banished it.

In any case it shouldn't make a difference either way. He'd been nice to her, for heaven's sake, that was all. And the last thing she needed right now was some ridiculous romantic interest. "Well…" She tried to summon a suitable reply; she didn't want a pity invitation, but to refuse seemed churlish after all he'd done.

"Of course, you said you wanted peace and quiet," Colin continued. "And my family definitely does not offer that.

Three-year-old twin terrors and a baby who does not stop screaming. Seriously." The smile he gave her was rueful, apologetic. He was offering her an escape route, a polite way to say no. And she should say no, because she really didn't want to be around babies, screaming or not, and being an add-on to Colin's happy family was far from appealing.

Yet somehow the words out of Anna's mouth were different. "I'd love to," she said. "Thank you." And the smile Colin gave her in response had her reminding herself quite forcefully that he was married, and he was simply being a Good Samaritan to a woman obviously in need.

After dinner, Colin stoked the fire for her, leaving a large pile of logs next to the wood stove so she wouldn't have to stumble about outside in the dark.

"If you like, I can give you a quick tour of the village tomorrow? Show you where the shop is?"

She should say no. She could manage on her own and Colin had his family to attend to. Anna doubted his wife would appreciate him ferrying a strange woman about town two days before Christmas.

"That's very kind of you, but I'm sure I'll be fine," she said, and Colin nodded.

"All right, then," he said. "If you need anything, you can just give a shout. I'm working on number four across the courtyard for most of the day."

"Oh." She liked the thought of him being near, stupidly enough. "Well. Thank you. For everything, I mean. I don't know what I would have done if you hadn't come to my rescue."

"Kipped on Frances' sofa, I expect," Colin answered with a wink. "And it's horribly lumpy, plus she has these awful cats that always jump on top of you the minute you sit down and dig their claws into your legs. They're evil, her cats."

Anna laughed. "I'd much rather be here, by the sounds of it."

He left soon after, and with his departure Anna felt as if the happiness and hope she'd been feeling, faint as they'd been, started to drain away.

Get a grip. And stop crushing on a near-stranger who just happened to help you.

She tidied up the dinner dishes and set out her sleeping bag and pillow in front of the stove. She couldn't remember the last time she'd actually camped. It must have been when she was about eight. Still, the house didn't feel quite so empty now that she had the fire going and there was milk in the fridge. It wasn't the holiday she'd anticipated, but maybe, she thought as she snuggled into the sleeping, just maybe, it would all work out after all.

Chapter Three

WHEN COLIN DROVE up to Willoughby Close at eight a.m. the next morning, Number One looked dark and empty. Then he noticed a lazy curl of smoke rising from the chimney and his heart lifted. At least Anna had kept the fire going all night.

He was tempted to knock on the door and ask how she was, but he resisted. He'd acted enough like a prat last night, brandishing the bottle of wine he'd bought from the post office and suggesting he take her on a tour of the village. She must think he was pathetic, chasing after the first woman who blew into town, and one who was obviously alone and vulnerable.

He hadn't meant it like that… at least, he didn't think he had. It was hard to know what his intentions were because there was no denying Anna was a beautiful woman. And when she'd smiled… Colin had been completely blindsided, dazzled by how utterly enchanting she'd looked. He'd like to convince himself he was just being a friendly handyman to a neighbor in need, but when his neighbor had sexy legs, a killer smile, and eyes he could happily lose yourself in, well, it was hard to know why he was doing what he was.

He'd keep his distance today, Colin decided as he un-loaded his tools from the back of the Rover. He didn't want to creep Anna out and, like she'd said, she wanted some peace and quiet to think things through.

He wondered how long it had been since her fiancé had broken it off. She'd certainly seemed cloaked in sorrow last night, and yet when she'd talked about her fiancé she'd been matter-of-fact. Colin hadn't detected the telltale lip wobble or glassy eyes of someone whose heart had been recently broken by a bloke. Or was that just wishful thinking?

He needed to stop thinking that way, full stop. She was recently broken up, alone in a strange place. The last thing he should consider was making a play. Besides, he wasn't a fling kind of bloke, much to his mates' disgust and his sisters' delight, although they sometimes accused him of being the dreaded serial monogamist. Colin didn't think that was fair, though; he was just determined to find the one, wherever she was, *who*ever she was. She wasn't, he was pretty sure, Anna Vere.

He spent the morning sanding floorboards in the third bedroom of Number Four, the largest cottage on the close. They were all looking pretty swish, if he said so himself, and Lady Stokely, the lone resident of Willoughby Manor, had seemed pleased by the plans, although she hadn't actually stopped by the cottages since Colin had begun the work. For all of the renovation work he'd dealt with her nephew Henry Trent, a London banker who was heir to the title and the house, and had been above board if a bit brisk in all of his conversations.

By midday he was trying to think of reasons to stop by Anna's cottage that wouldn't look obvious or desperate and annoyed with himself for thinking that way. He ate the sandwich he'd brought in his Rover, his back to Number One, determined to act normal. The sound of the front door opening had him almost swiveling in his seat, but he pretended to ignore it, sad tosser that he'd suddenly become.

Then he heard a rap on his window and, startled, he turned to see Anna smiling uncertainly at him from six inches away.

Hurriedly he rolled down the window. "Hey."

"Hi." Her smile deepened, and Colin felt that same whooshing rush of a response. She really had to stop doing that if he was going to stay sane. "How's your work going?"

"Fine. Just finishing off the upstairs floors." He studied her, trying not to be obvious about it.

She looked better than she had last night, pink-cheeked from the cold, her dark hair caught in a high ponytail. She wore a gray cable-knit sweater and another pair of skinny jeans, these ones in cream denim, which did amazing things to her legs. Of course, he was pretty sure her legs were already amazing. "You slept all right?"

"Surprisingly well." Another smile, and this time Colin

averted his eyes. A man could only take so much. "I don't think I've slept in a sleeping bag on the floor since I was a child."

"Really?"

What did that say about her? City girl, privileged upbringing? Everything he'd seen so far suggested it, and yet despite her air of expensive elegance she seemed surprisingly laidback. She'd been willing to rough it, after all, and hadn't remotely thrown a fit about the condition—and emptiness—of the cottage.

"I suppose you camp a lot?" she asked.

"As a kid, yeah. I was always setting up the tent in the back garden. Wanted my own space."

"From all those sisters?"

"Yep." He smiled and nodded, wanting to keep the conversation going but not sure how. "You have any? Siblings, I mean?"

"No, I'm an only child."

Her face clouded a little and Colin cursed himself for putting his foot in it. But how was he to know?

"Actually, I was wondering if you could point me in the direction of the village," she said, brightening again. "I thought of figuring it out by myself but I have a terrible sense of direction and I don't feel like wandering halfway to Oxford in this cold."

"Of course. It's not far. Just down the drive there, and then right and a quick left which gets you out to the main road. Then it's pretty easy, you take the second left past the village green…" Colin trailed off because Anna was shaking her head.

"Sorry, but when I said I had a terrible direction, I meant really terrible. Could I… could I take you up on your offer last night and have you show me?"

Colin tried to keep his expression merely friendly even though he felt like fist-pumping the air. "Sure," he said, his tone light, casual. "Not a problem at all."

ANNA HAD SLEPT in late thanks to jet lag, and woken up feeling surprisingly refreshed and even better, optimistic. Sunshine had streamed through the windows as she'd made herself a cup of tea—Colin had thoughtfully included an electric kettle in her box of provisions. She'd opened the French windows to the little terrace that overlooked rolling fields, breathing in the fresh, cold air. A low hedge separated her small garden from her neighbor's, and Anna imagined it could be quite friendly and cozy, living in this little close—assuming one got on with their neighbors. She wondered if the woman coming in the new year with her daughter was looking forward to it.

After breakfast, she took a long, hot bath, the tub living up to all of her expectations. Relaxed, she'd dressed and emerged, ready to explore. When she'd seen Colin sitting in his Land Rover she'd walked over without even thinking about it. She'd asked him to accompany her into the village in the same way, not second-guessing herself, just wanting his company. Was that desperate—or just nice?

In any case, here they were, strolling alone the rutted road they'd bumped along last night. In the bright sunlight Anna could see how lovely it all really was—woodland on one side and landscaped lawn on the other, leading to an impressive Elizabethan manor in the distance, the golden Cotswold stone gleaming in the winter sunlight.

She slowed as they approached the grand, sweeping drive, to have a good look. "Someone lives there?"

"Yes, Lady Stokely. Dorothy Madingley-Trent, to give her full name. She's a widow, about eighty years old. Kind of terrifying, actually."

"I'm sure. It was her idea to do up the old stables as cottages?"

"Her nephew's, I think, Henry Trent. He's a city type in London, investment banker, that kind of thing."

"Right." She knew that type all too well.

"I suspect they need a bit of cold, hard cash. The upkeep on Willoughby Manor has got to be enormous. And these titled families aren't swimming it anymore, not these days."

"No, I suppose not." They continued walking down the drive, towards the main road that led into the village. The air was cold and crisp, the sky a startling, bright blue. Anna felt invigorated, more than she had in a long time. She walked with her arms swinging at her sides, her stride brisk and purposeful, feeling as if she was finally going somewhere.

They followed the twists and turns of the main road into the village, the green in the distance, surrounded on three sides by quaint-looking cottages, the Christmas tree at its center. Anna paused to admire the view before following Colin to the high street.

"Frances said there was a river…"

"Yes, the Lea, a very small tributary of the Thames. It runs at the other end of the village, past the manor. A nice spot."

"It seems like a pretty village," Anna said as they headed down the high street, such as it was. In between terraced cottages were a few odd, homely-looking shops—a garage, a fish and chips takeaway, a vet, a secondhand shop with a window full of dusty antiques and a marmalade cat reigning over them all, a library, a bakery with trays of fresh-baked gingerbread in the window, and the post office shop that looked like the village's only source of groceries.

"It's all right," Colin said, a note of easy affection in his voice. "It's not as chocolate-box quaint as some of the places around here, with their organic farm shops and Burberry everywhere you look, flash SUVs on every corner, but it's a good, relaxed kind of place. Or at least it was. Lots of Londoners moving in here now, upping the property prices and turning one of the locals into some awful gastropub. Some kind of lentil stew was on the menu the last time I looked." He grimaced good-naturedly. "It had more of a salt of the earth feel when I was growing up. Bog-standard pints and fish and chips."

"And you chose to stay, obviously."

"Yes, never thought about going somewhere else, really. I always wanted to be where I knew people and people knew me, and so here I've stayed."

They'd reached the post office shop and Colin held the door open for her. "This is where you can get your basics, if you don't fancy living off takeaway."

Anna stepped inside, the bells on the door jangling merrily. The shop was tiny, with a counter for the post office in the back, and a couple of aisles of food by the till. A tiny LED Christmas tree perched by the cash register, and the woman at the till was wearing a Santa hat with jingle bells that made Anna smile.

She took in the basic packets of pasta and rice, jars of sauce and soup, and a very small selection of refrigerated items—milk, cheese, juice, and a few slightly withered apples and bananas. It would do.

"Sorry, it's not Waitrose," Colin murmured.

"Waitrose?"

"The upscale supermarket. You'll have to go to Witney for that."

"I'm fine with this. Do you mind if I load up a bit?"

"Not at all."

She spent an awkward yet also pleasant few moments browsing the limited selection, Colin by her side. After selecting some prepackaged ham, a jar of mustard, and a couple of unripe tomatoes, she gave Colin a quick smile and headed for the till. At least she'd figured out lunch. She'd come back tomorrow for the rest.

It was strange, but sorting out this makeshift, temporary life was kind of fun. Better, perhaps, than barricading herself in a bedroom overdone with chintz and bingeing on bad TV.

Her shopping finished, they headed outside into the crisp sunlight. Anna glanced up and down the street, noting the Christmas lights that been strung along the streetlamps, the sign in the post office window advertising a candlelight carol service on Christmas Eve.

"It's hard to believe Christmas is the day after tomorrow," she said.

"You don't mind spending it on your own?"

"Not this year." She'd been avoiding thinking about Christmas, about the kind of Christmas she'd envisioned in her future—stockings, presents, the big turkey dinner, snowball fights and singing carols. It all seemed sadly pointless now.

"Do you have some family Christmas traditions?" she asked as they started walking back. "Special things you do?"

Colin cocked his head, thinking. "Just the usual, I suppose. Lots of naff presents and too much food. Chocolate. My mum used to be keen on going to church."

"I saw there was a carol service tomorrow night." Too late she realized it sounded like a heavy-handed hint for an invitation.

"Yes, that's quite nice. We usually end up going, if we're organized, anyway." He brightened, as if the possibility had just occurred to him. "Why don't you come along with us?"

Anna murmured something noncommittal. She didn't really feel like tagging along Colin's happy family. In fact, she was starting to feel uncomfortable that he was spending so much time with her. He had to be well-known in the village. Would people gossip about him walking down the high street with a strange woman?

"You should get back to work, I'm sure," she said, quickening her step. "I've taken you away long enough."

"I don't mind. Always nice to have a change." Colin was ambling along slow and easy, seeming unhurried to get back to Number Four's floors.

"Still…" It had been so pleasant walking and chatting with Colin, she'd almost forgotten he was married. Guilt rushed through her, hot and prickly. "I don't want to keep you. You've been so kind." She was walking as quickly as she could now, practically tripping over her own feet. Colin touched her arm.

"Hey, is everything okay? You look a bit spooked."

"No…" She let out a laugh, high and uncertain. "I just don't want to be a burden. You've helped me out so much already."

"You're not a burden, Anna." His voice was low and sincere, and the way he said her name made her shiver inside.

Bad Anna. "I've enjoyed it, actually. Spending time with you, I mean."

"Right." She looked away, completely confused. Was she imagining the flirty vibe? Colin's hand was still on her arm, long, brown fingers wrapped gently around her wrist. She tingled where his fingertips brushed her bare skin.

"But maybe I'm being insensitive," Colin said with a little laugh. He released her arm. "My sisters always say I'm a bit of a blockhead that way. You told me you wanted to be on your own, and here I am, pushing in. Sorry. I'll leave you to it."

"It's not that…" Anna stared at him helplessly, wishing she could explain. But what could she say? *You're married and when I spend time with you I stupidly start to crush.* "I've enjoyed it, too," she said after a moment. "It's been… fun."

"Good." Colin nodded, looking pleased. His eyes crinkled at the corners, looking very blue in his weathered face. "So dinner is still on for tonight?"

There was no harm in spending time with his family, Anna reasoned. "Yes," she said firmly. "It is."

They walked back to Willoughby Close in companionable silence, and Colin went off to work while Anna made herself some lunch, stoked up the woodstove, and then decided to head out again to explore a bit more. Instead of walking towards the main road she turned left up the sweeping drive for a closer peek at Willoughby Manor. It was a surprisingly friendly-looking, stately home, with its mullioned windows winking in the winter sunlight. A box hedge in need of some serious pruning lined the front of the house, and the tall, carved wooden doors at the front were flanked by small yew trees. Anna stood to the side, curious to see more and yet not wanting to seem too nosy. Was Lady Stokely in residence? She wondered if the elderly lady was spending Christmas by herself, just as she was.

Quietly, her boots crunching softly on the gravel, Anna walked around to the back of the manor house. She could see a walled Victorian garden that must have once provided all the vegetables and fruit for the estate, and an orchard in the distance, the trees ancient and arthritic-looking, their twisted branches bent to the ground, the tufty grass littered with rotting apples.

Suddenly the back door opened, and an ancient-looking woman stood on the doorway, dressed in a voluminous white nightgown and black rubber boots, her white hair piled on top of her head. Her eyebrows drew together as she caught sight of Anna.

"May I help you?" she asked in the cut-crystal tones of the upper class.

"Sorry, I'm being incredibly nosy," Anna blurted. She was starting to blush. "I was just curious about the house. I'm staying in Willoughby Close."

Lady Stokely—for surely that was who she was—continued to frown. "Willoughby Close?"

"The stables, I mean. You're having them converted into

cottages?"

"Oh. Yes." Her expression cleared, her shoulders slumping slightly as she gazed into the wintry distance. "I suppose it will be nice to have neighbors. I didn't realize they were being let so soon."

"Oh, not until January," Anna explained. "I'm just staying through Christmas. I was meant to be in a bed and breakfast, but it got flooded."

"How unfortunate for you." Lady Stokely looked her up and down. "It will be a quiet Christmas here. I'll be lucky if my nephew manages to telephone." Her voice was touched with acid. "The misfortune of not having one's own children, you see. The obligation is so much less." She sighed and then turned back inside. "Feel free to wander, my dear. There is no one here but me to disturb you, and I shall be keeping warm in the only heated room in the house." With that rather dire announcement, she went back inside, closing the door behind her.

Anna stood there for a moment, shivering in the chilly breeze that had kicked up, wondering if she'd be like Lady Stokely one day, alone and lonely, albeit in a much smaller residence. Sighing, she turned and headed back towards Willoughby Close and the empty house that awaited her.

Chapter Four

ANNA HAD SPENT far too long debating what to wear for her dinner with Colin and his family. Jeans didn't quite seem appropriate, but the last thing she wanted to do was look like she'd gussied up too much. She settled on the only dress she'd packed, one of soft jersey in a deep magenta color, paired with a cashmere shrug to dress it down as well as keep warm.

Colin had said he'd pick her up at seven, and Anna was standing by the door at ten to, peering out at the darkness, feeling unaccountably nervous. How had he explained her to his family? She felt like such a stray.

The lights of his Land Rover cut a comforting swath through the darkness, and then he was hopping out and knocking on the door, looking rugged and only just scrubbed up in a pair of navy corduroys and a white button-down shirt. His hair, Anna saw, was still damp from a shower.

"You look nice," he remarked as he opened the passenger door for her. The footwell, Anna noted, had been cleaned of coffee cups and banana peels, although a crumpled map had been shoved in the corner.

As she shot him a smiling glance and a murmured thank you, she clocked the blatant male appreciation in his eyes with a twinge of unease. Colin didn't seem like a player, but then why did this feel so much like a date? Why was he looking at her the way a man looked at a woman?

"So where do you live?" she asked when they'd both gotten in and Colin was reversing down the track.

"Me?" He sounded surprised. "I live around the corner, down Mill Lane." He nodded towards the fields beyond Willoughby Manor. "That way. Bunch of old weavers' cottages there and I'm doing mine up. Have been for about five years." He turned out onto the main road, heading back into the village.

Anna glanced back at the darkness, the way he'd indicated he lived. "Aren't... aren't we going to your house?"

"My house?" Again with the note of surprise, which didn't make sense. "No. We're going to my sister's."

"Oh. Sorry, I just thought..." She paused, because she suddenly had the feeling she might have gotten the wrong end of the proverbial stick. The very wrong end.

"What did you think?" Colin slowed the Rover to glance at her, his eyes bright in the darkness.

"I thought... that is..." Anna stumbled over her words and then thought, *to hell with it.* "Are we having dinner with your family? I mean, your wife... and kids..."

"My wife?" Colin practically yelped the word. "I'm not married." He sounded appalled. "That is, I wouldn't mind being married, you know, someday, but I'm not... I'm single."

"Oh. Okay." Anna pressed her hands to her hot cheeks before dropping them as she realized how revealing the gesture was. "I just assumed when you mentioned the twins and the baby..."

"My sister's kids." He pretended to shudder. At least Anna thought it was pretend. "Thank God."

"Right." She looked out the window, trying to untangle her emotions.

The first one she isolated was relief that he was single. That the flirty vibe she'd picked up on was real and not wrong. Then she chastised herself for thinking that way because, really, she could not start something with Colin Heath. Not when she was in such a fragile state, and would be returning to New York in less than two weeks.

And yet... she was glad she wasn't about to walk in to Colin's happy home, watch him slide his arms around his adoring wife's waist as his toddlers tackled his knees. No, instead she'd be walking into Colin's sister's home, his nosy, bossy, older sister, as his... what? His date? The relief she felt began to trickle away. What had she gotten herself into?

"We're here." Colin pulled the Land Rover in front of a rambling farmhouse covered in ivy with Christmas lights draped haphazardly around the bushes and trees in front. "I should brief you a little," he added as he turned off the ignition. "This is Emma's house—she's my middle sister. She's like a mother hen, all clucking goodwill. Jane is the oldest—she's an academic living in Oxford, quite officious. Rose is the youngest—she lives in the village, too, and was just married last year. She works as a teacher at the primary school."

"Should I be scared?" Anna asked, only half-joking.

"Yes," Colin answered solemnly. "Terrified."

Too bad she didn't know if he was joking either.

COLIN HAD AN urge to reach for Anna's hand as they headed inside, but fortunately he suppressed it. She'd thought he was *married?* He was still kind of reeling from that one. Clearly they had not been on the same wavelength at all, a realization that shamed him a little.

He'd thought they'd shared a connection last night and on the walk today, but that seemed like it was just his wishful thinking. His *stupid* thinking, because this couldn't go anywhere. He barely knew her. But he'd enjoyed himself in the last twenty-four hours, more, perhaps, than he should admit, especially if she'd been operating under the false impression that he was already taken.

"Colin!"

Emma flung open the front door, all smiles and smelling of cinnamon and baby powder. "Here." She hugged him and thrust a baby at him at the same time, so Colin was left flailing, catching baby Will's drool on his cheek. He wiped it off with a grimace, noticing how Anna hid a smile.

"And you must be Anna," Emma said, and being Emma, she enveloped Anna in a hug who returned it awkwardly, looking bemused.

Maybe inviting her for dinner hadn't been such a good idea. His sisters were going to grill him about Anna endlessly, and he didn't even know what he was doing or why. He supposed it was hard to resist a beautiful damsel in distress.

"Come in, come in." Emma ushered them into the comfortable chaos of her kitchen—toddlers running amok, pots bubbling on top of the Aga, and Colin's two brothers-in-law standing in the doorway to the dining room, drinking beer. Colin looked around for someone to pass off the baby to so he could join them, but the only person with free hands was Anna.

"Would you mind…?" He was holding Will out like a bulky parcel with flailing legs when he noticed Anna's shocked look. She hadn't automatically reached up to take the baby, which was what most women did. Wasn't it?

"Of course," she murmured, a beat too late, and then she reached out to take Will.

She was more awkward with babies than he was, Colin noted as he gave her Will. Anna held the baby away from her body as if she wanted to avoid all body contact and then, looking extremely self-conscious, she perched him on her hip. Fortunately Will was used to being passed around and he gave Anna a big drooly, toothless grin and grabbed at her hair with one chubby hand.

Colin was accepting a bottle of Wychwood Ale from his brother-in-law, Tim, so he didn't notice Anna's reaction, but when he looked back at her after having taken a long swallow she looked rather bright-eyed. Kind of emotional.

"Is everything okay?" he asked in a low voice.

"Fine." The smile she gave him was brittle, as if it could crack. "Everything's fine."

Colin hesitated, because everything was clearly not fine, but he didn't know how to insist graciously that Anna tell him what the heck was going on. Anna adjusted Will on her hip, the baby now patting her nose experimentally, and she walked towards the kitchen, effectively turning her back on him.

"May I help?" she asked Emma, and amidst a flurry of introductions, Emma told her she was already helping by holding the baby.

Colin watched Anna get swallowed up in the Borg-like entity of his family and wondered if he'd imagined that weird, tense moment when he'd handed her Will.

ANNA WAS TRYING really hard to hold it together. She thought she was almost managing it. But then baby Will would grin at her, or nuzzle against her chest, smearing drool across her dress, and her composure started to slip again. In a moment she'd be bawling. She hadn't been with babies since the operation. She'd avoided her friends with newborns, knowing it was mean but recognizing how much—or how little—she could handle.

Four months was not long enough to heal that kind of heartbreak. She'd looked away from strollers in the street and averted her eyes from the big, round pregnant bellies that suddenly seemed to be sprouting up everywhere, as if the entire world was in a joyful, fecund state except for her.

Part of her reason for coming to England was to avoid the whole kids-at-Christmas thing. Children seemed to come out of the woodwork at holidays, and to prove it, here she was with an actual baby in her arms.

He smelled so good, like baby powder and apples. She had the urge to bury her nose in his neck and breathe in deeply but she had a feeling that would look a little weird. People said babies were cute enough to eat but they didn't actually mean it.

Colin's sisters were moving around her with brisk officiousness, seeming to compete with each other in who could be most helpful. Anna stayed out of the way, clutching Will and trying not to lose it.

"So how did Colin meet you, exactly?" Jane asked.

She looked every inch the academic, wearing a crisp blouse and pencil skirt, her dark hair drawn back into a neat ponytail, her lips pursed as she whisked Yorkshire pudding batter into an eggy froth.

"I'm staying in Willoughby Close, in one of the cottages he's been renovating."

"Oh, Willoughby Close, right." Jane nodded, sounding dismissive. "He's actually managed to complete that project, has he?"

Now what did *that* mean? "There's a bit of tile to finish on the upstairs bath," she said uncertainly, and Jane nodded, as if Anna had just confirmed all of her worst suspicions.

"Colin always means well, doesn't he?" she remarked to no one in particular, and Anna prickled.

She was starting not to like Jane.

"Give it a rest, Jane," Emma called good-naturedly over her shoulder. "Just because Colin didn't finish your kitchen refit." She turned to Anna with a conspiratorial smile. "She kept changing her mind about every little detail, wanted Spanish tile and then ceramic, drove Colin mad. In the end he said he wasn't going to do it anymore, not until she kept to one thing."

"Oh. Right." Anna smiled back, feeling strangely comforted.

"Listen, you wouldn't mind giving that little monster his bottle, would you? It's his bedtime."

"Oh? Um..." Anna looked down at Will's face, starting to feel panicked.

"I weaned him a couple of weeks ago," Emma confided as she made up a bottle of formula. "I know they say a year but I have three-year-old twins. There are limits." She handed Anna the bottle. "Just stick it in his mouth and he'll do the rest. It's quiet in the lounge if you go through. You can have a moment of peace and quiet. Colin will bring you a drink."

"Okay," Anna said, because what else could she say?

She squeezed through the press of husbands by the door and found the lounge, a comfortable room with squashy sofas, a thick pile rug, and huge fireplace. Positioning herself in a deep armchair by the fire, she awkwardly maneuvered Will to the crook of her arm. He saw the bottle and smacked his lips.

"Hungry, huh?" Anna said.

Her chest was starting to feel tight with too much emotion. Carefully she put the bottle in Will's mouth, and just like Emma had said, he knew what to do. He grabbed it with both hands and began drinking greedily, a blissed-out look on his little face that made Anna smile through the pain.

Heaven help her, this hurt. She took a deep breath, blinking back tears, and tried to enjoy the heavy, warm weight of the baby in her arms, the contented sounds of his suckling, and the lights of the enormous Christmas tree that sparkled and shone. The air smelled of roast beef and cinnamon.

How did I get here? She felt overwhelmed by the crowd of Colin's family, friendly and yet as nosy and bossy as he'd warned her about, and blindsided by the baby in her arms, the one situation she would have done anything to avoid. But she had to get used to this sometime. She couldn't avoid children forever; she didn't even want to. But it felt too soon. It hurt too much.

"A glass of mulled wine coming right up," Colin said as he came into the lounge bearing a glass of spicy red wine with an orange slice floating in it.

"Sounds delicious. I haven't had that before."

"A Christmas necessity in England, along with mince pies."

"Yes, the pub promised something about that."

"Of course. We'll have those after." He put the glass on the table next to the chair, frowning slightly as he looked down at her. "Are you sure you're okay?"

Anna tried to smile. "Why do you keep asking me that?"

"I don't know. You just looked a little…" He waved hand and Anna raised her eyebrows.

"A little…?"

"Emotional."

Ah. Well, that was because she was. "Just the jet lag catching up with me," she said without meeting his eyes.

Will was finishing the dregs of his bottle, his lips slack, forming a perfect rosebud, his eyelids fluttering. Gently, Anna eased the bottle from his mouth and instinctively brought his body closer to hers. He nestled in naturally, causing another pang to go through her.

"You have a knack," Colin said softly. "You'll be a great

mum one day, I'm sure."

It was an innocent comment, artlessly made, and yet it felt as if he'd just sunk a knife through her chest. She let out a choked sound and then took a deep breath, desperate to steady herself. She could not fall apart here, among all these strangers. She just couldn't.

"Anna...?" Colin put a hand on her shoulder and Anna bent her head, her hair swinging forward to hide her face.

Tears pressed against her lids, a near-overwhelming pressure. *Get a grip, Anna. Just get a grip!*

"Has my little man fallen asleep?" Emma appeared in the doorway, a dish towel in one hand. "Would you mind popping him upstairs, Anna? Second door on the left."

Actually, she would mind, but at least it gave her an excuse to be alone for a few minutes. She knew Emma was trying to make her feel welcome and involved by handing her Will, but not everyone wanted to cuddle a baby. And while part of Anna had enjoyed holding and feeding Will—too much—another part, the greater part, had felt like it was the worst kind of torture. At least now he was asleep it would end. She only had the rest of the evening to get through.

Carefully she rose from the chair and brushed past Colin to make for the stairs. At least it was peaceful upstairs, away from the din of Colin's family. She found the nursery, the smallest bedroom in the back of the house with lots of blue and stenciled elephants cavorting on the walls. As Anna approached the crib, Will let out a sigh and snuggled against her. She drew in a shuddering breath. She could do this.

Gently, so gently, she laid him in the crib. His eyelids fluttered and his mouth screwed up and Anna tensed, bracing herself for a sudden shriek, but then his eyes closed completely and his face relaxed. He was asleep. Letting out a breath of relief, she stepped slowly away from the crib.

"Anna."

She nearly let out a yelp as she bumped into Colin who had come into the room behind her. He put his hands on her shoulders to steady her and for a second Anna wanted to stay there, almost leaning against him, the solid strength of his body behind her, his palms warm, even through the fabric of her dress.

"Sorry," he whispered. "I didn't mean to scare you."

She shook her head, pressing a finger to her lips and, twisting away from him, slipped out of the room. Colin followed, closing the door quietly behind him.

"I feel like I've upset you somehow," he said.

He was searching her face, his blue, blue eyes creased at the corners, and Anna shook her head again, wanting, needing to deny it. But then Colin pressed his thumb against her cheek, the caress shocking her to her core. He drew his hand away.

"Tears," he said softly. "You *are* upset."

"No…" Yet how could she deny it?

She sighed and rubbed her hands over her face, wishing she had more of a hold on her composure.

"Anna, please. Tell me what's going on."

"I'm not good with babies," she blurted. She dropped her hands and saw how comically perplexed he looked. "Or children. I'm just… not."

"Sorry, I didn't realize…"

"No, you wouldn't." Her voice came out more sharply than she'd intended and she sighed again. "Sorry, it's a long story and not one I can handle telling tonight, not with everyone downstairs waiting…" And wondering.

And probably making jokes about her and Colin and who knew what. Suddenly she couldn't stand any of it. The comforting warmth of the kitchen that had seemed so welcoming when she'd first come in now felt like a stifling prison. She'd have to endure hours of making chitchat, trying to prevaricate, dodging nosy questions, and she really didn't know if she had the strength.

"Look, I think this was a bad idea on my part," Colin said. He took her elbow and started moving them both down the stairs. "I'll run into the kitchen and tell Emma we're eating at the pub."

"What?" Anna stared at him in astonishment. "You can't—"

"Why can't I? Frankly, I'd prefer it and I think you would, too. Whatever is going on, you don't need my bossy sisters poking their noses into it."

"They'll be offended—"

"They'll get over it. And who cares, anyway?" He

shrugged, smiling. "I don't, and you shouldn't either. I'll tell them now," Colin said firmly. "You wait here."

Anna stood by the front door, feeling both awkward and hopeful, as Colin went into the kitchen. She heard the low, authoritative murmur of his voice, and then a chorus of surprised exclamations and protests. Colin spoke again; there were a few murmurs back, and then silence. Anna closed her eyes. What on earth could his family be thinking of her? She'd been here for all of fifteen minutes.

"That's sorted, then," he said as he came down the hallway, and then he took her arm. "Let's go to the pub."

Buoyant with relief and yet also struggling with apprehension, Anna followed him out the door.

Chapter Five

COLIN DIDN'T KNOW what had happened back at his sister's, but he felt in his gut that it had been the right decision to take Anna away. She'd looked so distraught and yet trying to hide it when she'd held Will. It made Colin wonder. Was she baby-phobic, or was it something deeper and more painful? He was determined not to press.

He snuck a glance at her in the passenger seat of his Rover, her pale face turned towards the window.

"What did you end up telling your family?" she asked, sounding subdued.

"I told them I was sweeping you away for a romantic dinner. That silenced them." He spoke lightly, meaning it as a joke, or at least sort of, but Anna looked startled.

"Don't worry," Colin said. "They're taken care of."

"Okay." She let out a soft, uncertain laugh. "You must think I'm—" She stopped, shaking her head, and he wondered how she meant to finish that thought.

He decided to do it himself. "I don't think anything. It was an awkward, overwhelming situation. I shouldn't have tossed you in it."

"I wouldn't say toss…"

"Still." They'd reached the pub and Colin pulled into the car park. "Now let's have a proper and quiet meal. If that's all right?" He glanced at her in the darkness; she was facing the window, her hair falling darkly against one pale cheek.

She turned to him, her smile fleeting and sweet. "That sounds perfect."

The pub was crowded and dim as Colin pushed his way through to get to the bar, nodding helloes to various acquaintances and friends and ignoring their speculative and openly curious looks when they caught sight of Anna. Most of them were probably wondering what he was doing with such a good-looking woman.

"What would you like?" he asked Anna, who had followed closely behind him, hugging her arms to herself, looking lost in the crowd of jolly pre-Christmas drinkers.

"Um… white wine, I guess. Thank you."

He ordered her wine and his pint, paid for both, and then shouldered his way back through the crowd to a small table tucked into a corner of the restaurant area.

"Here you are," he said, handing the glass of wine to her with a flourish. "This is a simple place, but it's got good food. If you want something fancier, you'll have to go to the Three Bells down the road."

"The gastropub you mentioned earlier?"

"Yep. Not my style."

"And this is The Drowned Sailor," Anna remarked as she looked around the pub with its ancient, blackened beams and various tatty sailing gear tacked onto the wall. "A bit grim, but I like it." She took a sip of wine, a smile lurking behind the uncertainty in her eyes. "Cheers."

"Cheers."

They sipped in silence for a few minutes, the scrum of the pub a comfortable, cheerful clamor around them.

Finally Anna put her glass down. "So you must be wondering why I went all…" She gestured with her hand. "You know."

"Like I said, it was an overwhelming situation."

"Yes, but…" She bit her lip, eyes downcast, lashes fanning her porcelain cheeks.

Clearly there was something more going on. Some past trauma? Did he want to know?

"You don't have to tell me anything," Colin said.

He felt both curious and apprehensive. What if he couldn't deal with whatever secret Anna was obviously keeping?

She looked a little taken aback by his hurried assurance. "Okay," she said after a tiny, brittle pause, and then she plucked the plastic menu stuck between the salt and pepper shakers and began to peruse it, her expression closed.

He'd blown that, clearly. Colin took a gulp of his beer. He hadn't meant to put her off, but…

"Sorry," he said into the silence. "I was only trying to say

I don't want to push you into telling me something you don't want to. But if you want to say…" He trailed off, at a loss.

He'd never been good with these emo-type conversations. No one in his family was. They pushed all the difficult stuff down, burying it deep, and moved on, bright smiles in place, the happy family with just a few telling absences.

"I don't know." Anna shrugged as she let out a shaky laugh. "It's not worth raking it all up again, I suppose." She looked up with a bright smile, as artificial as a sun lamp. "What are you going to order? Any recommendations?"

Should he push her to say something more, or would that be obnoxious? Colin had no idea. Truth be told, he was a little relieved not to talk about it, even though he was curious.

"The fish and chips are pretty good," he said after a beat. "Or the steak and ale pie."

"Fish and chips it is, then." She put the menu down and began to look at the pub with an affected, interested air that made Colin inwardly wince; it was so fake. But she was trying.

"I don't think that came out right before," he said, and she glanced at him, startled, caught in the headlights of his ineptitude.

"Sorry…?"

"I only meant, I wasn't trying to put you off before, but I think I did. I understand something was going on back there, Anna. I didn't mean to dismiss it." There. That was the best he had.

She stared at him for a long moment, her lower lip caught between her teeth, her eyes a deep, blue-gray and heartbreakingly wide. And then the waitress came to take their order.

Anna ordered the fish and chips and Colin bumbled through his order and then the waitress thankfully left them alone. Had the moment passed, or…?

"I'm infertile," Anna blurted.

Colin stared. "I… sorry. I'm so sorry. That is…" He was definitely out of his depth.

Infertile? Did that mean she'd tried for a baby or… what? He had no idea.

Anna let out a shaky laugh as she passed a hand over her face. "Goodness, that came out sounding wrong. I mean it's true, but…" Another, shakier laugh. "I didn't have to blurt it out like that. Sorry."

"Now we're both apologizing."

"It's just…" She dropped her hand, her gaze becoming clouded and distant. "Sometimes it feels like this lead weight pressing down on my chest, or this neon sign blaring over my head and only I can see it. I feel like if I *don't* say something, I'm almost lying. Is that weird?"

"I… I don't know," Colin admitted, because he definitely didn't. "But I think there's no wrong or right way to feel in this kind of situation."

She sat back with a sigh, seeming somewhat satisfied with his answer. "I guess not. But... anyway." She shook her head, as if to dismiss the whole subject. "It's all relatively recent for me and holding a baby... Will... it brought home the realization that I'll never hold one of my own. So." She pasted on a bright smile and reached for her wine.

Colin was silent for a moment, trying to figure out the most helpful response. He had no clue, so he decided honesty was best. Hopefully, anyway.

"I can't imagine how you're feeling, but I know how hard it is when life doesn't turn out the way you expect." He paused, laying his hands flat on the table, feeling for the words. "You have this whole picture in your head of how things are going to turn out and when they don't..." He felt a tightness in his chest and now he was the one trying to pass off a shaky laugh.

Anna's face had softened in sympathy, lush mouth downturned, eyes shadowed. "What happened?" she asked quietly.

Colin shrugged. "I was going to go into business with my father. 'Heath and Son', we'd talked about it for years, since I was a lad, really. Builders, the two of us, our own firm. My father worked as a construction foreman but he always wanted to be his own man. He said I had the guts for it, and so after I left uni we started up, right here in Wychwood. He died of a massive heart attack on the first job we did, only a couple of weeks after we'd signed all the documents, made

Heath & Son official." His mouth twisted and he looked down at his hands. "Not the way any of us saw things happening. He was only fifty-four."

"Oh, Colin." Anna reached out and laid one soft, slender hand over his. "I'm so sorry. I can't imagine how difficult that must have been."

"Sorry, wasn't trying to steal your thunder. Just wanted to say I can relate a little bit. Life is hard, sometimes."

"I know." Her smile was soft and sad and she squeezed his hand. "I know."

And despite the tightness in his chest and the lump of emotion that had taken residence in his throat, that touch of her hand on his had Colin feeling something else entirely. Desire, a sudden, hot rush. Totally inappropriate, but also rather wonderful. Colin gave her a sheepish smile, wondering if she knew what he felt or if he dared think she felt the same, at least a little bit.

Anna smiled back, self-conscious, and removed her hand. So, maybe not. Colin tried not to feel too disappointed. He was an ordinary bloke, not bad-looking but nothing special, a bit of a clod when it came to emotions and fashion sense, but he knew his way around a hammer and saw. Anna Vere, with her elegant beauty and her stylish clothes, her sense of quiet stillness, was way out of his league.

Anna took another sip of wine—her glass was almost

empty—to hide the sense of disquiet that had come over her. It felt as if everything was speeding up, happening way too fast. Yesterday, she'd been swaying on her feet, staring at a flooded room, and now she was practically holding hands after having a heart-to-heart with a man she could no longer say she barely knew. *What was happening?*

Maybe she'd completely embarrassed herself by blurting her issues out like that. Colin might be appalled. Mark had certainly got tired of what he viewed as her complaining.

And yet... Colin hadn't *seemed* appalled. A bit surprised, maybe, but he'd shared his own story. That had to mean something.

"What about your mom?" she asked. "I didn't see her at your sister's..." Of course, she'd barely been introduced before she'd been handed a baby and then nearly broken down.

Colin made a grimacing sort of face. "After Dad died she sold up—we had a farmhouse on the edge of the village—and bought a place in Portugal. She spends most of her time there now, and just comes for flying visits. She says there are too many memories here, but the fact is *we're* here. All her kids." He made another face, a sort of guiltily apologetic look. "I know, I know, I probably sound bitter. But it's like she just gave up on her family." He shrugged and took a sip from his pint.

"No, I can see how that would be hard. Like a double loss."

"Yes." Colin nodded. "Exactly."

Their meals arrived and they both dug in, eating in a surprisingly companionable silence. "What about your parents?" Colin asked after a little while. "Are they still around?"

"Yes, my parents are lovely. I'm an only child, though, and I came late in their lives, their little miracle they like to say." She smiled wryly. "So while it's great, sometimes it gets a bit... intense. I didn't want to do the whole Christmas thing this year because I knew they'd be fussing over me so much, wondering how I am, if I'm coping." She sighed, guilt niggling her again. "I probably broke my mother's heart."

"You've got to make your own choices though, haven't you? If they'll let you. My sisters still treat me like a little boy, but I'm thirty-six."

"I'm thirty-five," Anna answered with a smile, "and my parents sometimes act like I'm sixteen. My mother still wants me to bring my laundry home at holidays so she can iron it properly."

Colin laughed and nodded. "That's how my sisters are with me. Jane's licked her finger and given me the spit bath more than once, and I'm not talking about when I was a kid."

Anna laughed at that, a genuine laugh, from her belly, the kind she hadn't had in a long time. "Oh, dear. Do you think they'll ever let you grow up?"

Colin raised his glass. "Here's hoping."

"I always wanted brothers or sisters. You're lucky, you know, even if you don't feel like it."

"I know I am, really. Family's important, even when they drive you mad."

"Yes." A pang assailed her and she tried to ignore it.

It was so unhelpful, so pointless, to have the running commentary going in her head. *Family's so important and you'll never have your own.* Mark had found it all so tedious. Even *she* had found it tedious after awhile, and yet it was impossible to stop.

"So, may I ask," Colin began after a moment, "if the fiancé breakup had to do with…?"

"Yes, in a matter of speaking. Mark, my fiancé, didn't actually mind that I couldn't have children. He hadn't really wanted them, something I should have realized but somehow didn't. Because you should talk about that, don't you think, before you get engaged? Make sure you're on the same page?"

"Yes, I'd think so."

"Do you want children?" she asked, genuinely curious, and only realized after how it sounded. As if she thought they… "Sorry, I was just wondering."

"No, it's fine." Colin smiled easily. "I always thought I'd have a few, bung them in the back of the Rover along with the dog. Black Lab." He rubbed his jaw thoughtfully. "Just hasn't happened yet."

"It still could." A thought which gave her a stupid pang.

"Yes, although I suppose I'm getting up there, aren't I? Forty's on the horizon."

Anna laughed. "Four years away!"

"Still." He paused, turning his empty pint glass in circles between his callused palms. "I was engaged a couple of years ago, to a woman named Laura. Local, like me. We got as far as planning the wedding, even booking the church."

"What happened?" Anna asked quietly, her breath caught in her chest.

"We didn't have that talk you mentioned. Not about kids, we knew we both wanted those eventually, but about life. Expectations and all that. I was happy to trundle along, the son in Heath & Son, but she wanted more. Bigger house, I guess, posher village. Who knows? She kept pushing me to be something I wasn't. When she realized I didn't want to change she left." He shrugged, philosophical now. "Better before we said the vows than after, eh?"

"Yes, but it must have been hard."

"It was, but not in the way I expected. My heart wasn't broken, and that made me realize that I probably shouldn't have got engaged at all."

"Yes, I suppose that's how I felt about Mark," Anna said slowly, searching for the words. "My heart wasn't broken, not by him leaving anyway. The infertility was a much bigger deal to me than losing Mark."

"But if he didn't want kids, why did you break up?"

Anna sighed. "He couldn't stand what he called my

moping. He thought I should get over it, and quickly. Really, it made everything simpler, according to him." Her throat tightened, the old hurt flared hotly once again. "I think that was the end, when he said that. *Simpler.*"

"He sounds like a right prick, if you don't mind me saying so."

Anna laughed, the hurt she'd been holding tightly inside starting to loosen. "I don't mind."

"Good." Colin smiled at her, and she smiled back, and the moment spun out and started morphing into something else, something that made Anna's skin prickle and her heart beat a little harder. Stupid to feel this way, and yet it felt so *nice,* parts of her waking up that had been dormant for a long time.

"I think I've shared more with you than I have with anyone else," she said with a little laugh.

Her handful of work friends were always busy, busy and her friends from college had never liked Mark. Friends with children she'd avoided completely.

"Likewise," Colin admitted. "Not a bad thing, though, is it?" His blue gaze rested on her thoughtfully, making her feel warm.

A girl could read a lot into that gaze. Too much.

"No, it's not a bad thing," Anna agreed, because it wasn't.

And nice as it was, it was also strange. She'd known Colin for twenty-four hours and yet she felt comfortable with him. He felt familiar, but it was more than that. The way his eyes creased when he smiled, the big, capable hands circling his pint glass... they made a shiver of longing go through her. She could imagine those big hands on her body. Those eyes smiling down at her as he kissed her... She could imagine it and she wanted it.

Appalled at how quickly her thoughts had spiraled out of control, Anna looked away, fighting a flush. The restaurant area of the pub was emptying out, and the bar was becoming crowded with people who seemed determined to drink until Christmas. But it was a friendly crowd, lots of good-natured joking, laughter, and smiles. Christmas carols played in the background, tinny and cheerful.

"We should probably go," Anna said. "What time is it?"

"Just gone nine. I'll drive you home." He got up, sliding his wallet out of his back pocket, and Anna scrabbled for her purse.

"Let me—"

"Absolutely not," Colin said firmly, and Anna sat back, knowing he was the kind of man who would insist on paying.

"Then thank you very much."

"You're welcome." He gave her a quick smile that made that shiver go through her again.

Was she playing with fire? She wasn't a fling kind of girl. She'd had precisely two relationships in her entire life—Ian, a moody boy in college, and Mark, the flash city slicker.

Casual sex had never been on her agenda, and she had a gut feeling that embarking on it now, no matter how tempted she was, would be a disaster. She was feeling vulnerable, way too close to bursting into tears at inopportune moments or reading too much into casual gestures. She could *not* have a fling with Colin Heath.

"Ready?" He appeared at their table, eyebrows raised in expectation.

Anna stood up. "Yes. Thanks again."

"My pleasure, Anna. Seriously." His warm gaze rested on her for another moment and Anna swallowed.

Reminded herself about the not-having-a-fling thing. Not, of course, that Colin was even interested. He might be single and sexy and sweet but she'd basically shown herself to be a basket case at every opportunity.

They headed out to his Rover and drove back to Willoughby Close in thoughtful, comfortable silence. Colin had just turned into the courtyard in front of the cottages when he swore under his breath. Anna looked at him in surprise, and then she clocked the navy blue Jaguar parked in front of Number One. Someone else, it seemed, had taken residence in Willoughby Close.

Chapter Six

THIS WAS NOT a good end to what had been a promising and pleasurable evening. "Wait here," Colin instructed Anna, and then climbed out of the Rover, steeling himself to deal with Henry Trent, Lord Stokely-in-waiting.

Henry climbed out of his Jag, his patrician face drawn in disapproving lines. He was only thirty-four, two years younger than Colin, but he acted decades older, wearing the responsibility as the only heir with heavy dignity.

"Henry." At least Trent didn't put on lord-of-the-manor airs. He'd always told Colin to call him by his first name like a normal bloke, and treated Colin the same.

"Colin. My aunt rang me today to say someone had taken up residence in Willoughby Close?"

"Yes, just through Christmas." Colin tried to sound relaxed even though he could tell Henry wasn't pleased by this development. "Her room at a local B&B had flooded and she had nowhere to stay."

Henry's mouth tightened. "I would have appreciated being asked about this. The cottages are not a charity."

Colin kept his smile. "It's Christmas."

"You realize the difficulty in having someone stay?" Henry asked in his level, lawyer's voice. "Squatter's rights—"

"Trust me, she's not a squatter. She's American—"

"Damage to the property—"

"I'll fix any damage, free of charge."

"Not to mention liability," Henry continued relentlessly. "If she injures herself while on the property, my aunt could be liable."

"She doesn't seem like the type to sue—"

Henry shook his head. "I'm sorry, Colin, but this was not approved and I cannot countenance it." He sounded regretful—and very firm. "She'll have to go somewhere else. Is she a friend of yours?" He nodded towards Anna's shadowy form in the front of the Rover. "Why can't she stay with you?"

"Ah, well." Now did not seem the right time to admit Anna was a complete stranger, or had been yesterday. "Henry, honestly, she's really not doing any harm—"

"I'm sorry." Henry's tone was final. "The cottages are not a free B&B, not even at Christmas."

Even in the darkness, Colin could see how set Henry's expression was. He needed to back down, especially if he wanted any more work at Willoughby Manor to come his way, which he most certainly did. He should have asked Henry first, but he'd been afraid of something like this and he hadn't expected the London lawyer to come down at

Christmas.

"Right," he said heavily. "Sorry. I'll clear her things out tonight."

"Good." Henry turned back to his Jaguar. "I'm staying at the manor for Christmas," he said, and Colin knew what the real message was. *I'll be watching.*

"Right. Enjoy the holiday with your aunt."

He stood there, smiling with effort, as Henry climbed in his Jaguar and drove away with a squeal of tires on gravel. Then Colin turned back to the Rover and Anna. What on earth was he going to tell her?

Slowly he opened the door and climbed inside. Anna turned to him with wide, anxious eyes. "Who was that? What's happened?"

"That was Henry Trent, the heir to Willoughby Manor. Somehow he got wind you were here."

"Oh." Anna bit her lip. "I went for a walk this afternoon and saw his aunt. She seemed friendly, in a stern, upper class sort of way. Should I not have said…?"

Colin sighed. "It doesn't matter."

"I'm not supposed to be in the cottage?"

"I didn't think it was a big deal, but Henry is finicky, always counting on the worst case scenario. He's afraid you'll sue his aunt for all she's got if you stub your toe on the stairs."

"Oh, but I wouldn't…"

"You and I know that." Colin started the car. "I'm afraid

Henry is determined that you not stay here."

"Oh." Anna's voice sounded hollow. "Well…"

"You could stay at Emma's," he continued as he weighed the options. "She's got a spare bedroom. I know it's not ideal, but…" He could see how unideal it was by the stricken expression on Anna's face. He took a deep breath, not quite meeting her eyes. "The other option is you could stay at mine. I have a spare bedroom, too, so…" He was starting to blush, damn it. What was he, sixteen? "I mean, as long as you didn't find it too weird or I don't know, awkward…" He trailed off. Could he possibly dig a bigger hole for himself?

"Um, okay." Nervously Anna tucked her hair behind her ears, looking anywhere but at him.

Should he reassure her that he wouldn't put the moves on? As much as he knew he wanted to?

"I know we don't know each other very well," he continued, his voice suddenly sounding too loud in the confines of the car, "but I assure you I'm trustworthy and I've got clean sheets. On the *spare* bed." He clarified quickly, and then closed his eyes. *Good Lord.* He was such an idiot. "Of course. I mean, of course the spare bed." *Stop. Just stop.*

"Right."

He thought he saw a smile lurking in her eyes, playing at the corners of her mouth, and he dared to smile back. Maybe they'd laugh about this eventually.

"Actually, I feel like I know you rather well," she confessed, "after all the soul-baring we did at the pub."

She sounded wry but he could see she was blushing, just as he was. They were as awkward as a couple of teenagers on a first date.

"I know what you mean." Dare he hope she was going to say yes...?

In that moment, Colin really wanted Anna to stay. And he wouldn't try it on. Well, not unless she came at him naked and willing, arms open wide, lips curved in a smile of blatant invitation...

That was an image he did not need in his head right at this moment.

"I'd rather stay with you," Anna said quietly. "If you don't mind."

"I don't." Relief poured through him, a cold, sweet rush. He felt *elated.* Smiling at her, he turned off the car. "Why don't we pack up your stuff and get going?"

THE WHOLE THING felt incredibly surreal as Anna packed up her suitcase—she hadn't unpacked much in any case—and Colin loaded the camping stuff back into the box he'd brought it in. She was actually staying with him. In his house. In his bed. His spare bed, she reminded herself, and a smile curved her mouth as laughter lit up her insides, just from remembering the way Colin had bumbled through his invitation. He could be so endearing sometimes. So lovable.

The word floated into her head like a bubble and then abruptly popped. *Lovable? Get a grip, Anna. You barely know this guy. If you weren't hurting so much, you wouldn't be thinking this way.* Dreaming impossible dreams just because her life had dive-bombed so spectacularly in recent months. She had to keep a hold on reality, which was that a man she barely knew was doing her a favor.

"Anna?" Colin's voice floated up the stairs. "Are you ready?"

"Yes." She zipped her suitcase and was about to haul it down the stairs when Colin appeared at the top and took it from her. Of course.

"I'll load all this into the Rover and then we can go." He tilted his head, his blue gaze sweeping searchingly over her. "You're sure you're okay with this?"

"Yes, I'm fine." She smiled back at him. "But if you keep asking me, I might start to wonder if you're some secret serial killer."

His grin was devastating. "You can check all my cupboards for dead bodies."

"You'd be a very stupid serial killer if you kept the bodies in your cupboards," Anna told him as they headed downstairs. "I should look for a buried pit or something in the back garden."

"You're the expert?"

"I've watched enough thrillers and episodes of *CSI*."

"No pits, promise."

They were outside, their breath creating little, frosty puffs in the still night air. The sky was endlessly black, lit only by a few pinpricks of stars and a sliver of moon. Anna glanced at the cute courtyard and the four cottages, all waiting for their prospective tenants to liven the place up. For a second she pictured the place as it might be in a couple of months, curtains at all the windows, bright flowers in the pots outside, the little courtyard ringing with chatter and laughter.

"I'll miss this place," she said with a little laugh. "It was pretty."

"At least there are a few more mod-cons at mine."

She was kind of curious about where Colin lived, Anna realized as she climbed back into the Land Rover. Would it be the typical bachelor pad, a big, battered leather sofa and an even bigger TV and not much else? She hoped not. But considering he was a man and his car was pretty messy, she supposed she should keep her expectations low. At least he'd promised her clean sheets.

They drove away from the village, down a narrow lane that wound its way next to the small but swift-flowing Lea River. A row of tumbledown cottages that looked like something out of an Austen adaptation appeared, all of them crammed together higgledy-piggledy, and Colin parked in front of the last one. Anna peered out the window at the two-story cottage of golden Cotswold stone, its chimney crooked and its blue-painted shutters askew, and fell in love.

"What an adorable place," she exclaimed.

Colin winced. "Please do not use the word adorable in anything that describes me or my possessions," he said with a long-suffering smile. "My sisters used that word all too often when I was growing up. There are incriminating photos of me dressed up in a tutu and sparkly tiara. Jane threatens to get them out for my wedding."

Anna laughed. "I'd like to see those."

Colin grabbed her suitcase out of the back and then unlocked the door, stepping aside so Anna could go in first. She walked under a low stone lintel into a small stone-flagged hall cluttered with welly boots, none of which seemed to match. She blinked in the darkness, one hand fumbling for a light, when something substantial barreled into her legs, sending her stumbling back against Colin with a startled *oof.*

His hand slipped around her waist to steady her, drawing her up against his hard chest. For a second Anna was more conscious of the feel of the length of Colin's powerful body against hers than the furry creature butting its head insistently against her legs.

"Sorry," Colin said, "that would be Millie." His mouth was close to her ear and his breath sent delicious shivers skittering down her spine. She had a strong desire never to move again.

"Millie…" She prompted, her voice unsteady.

Colin didn't seem inclined to move either. She could smell his aftershave, something woodsy and clean, and she knew if she turned her head her lips would brush his jaw. She was very tempted to do so; she could already imagine the gentle abrasion of his stubble against her lips.

"My black lab."

His arm was still around her waist, the top of it grazing her breasts, making sparks zip through her body as if she'd become electrically charged.

"I thought your black lab was theoretical," she said, "along with the children you were going to bung in the back of your Rover."

"Nope, Millie is real." His breath tickled her ear. "But the kids aren't. Yet." A rather stark reminder that as delicious as it felt to be held by Colin Heath, their relationship—if she could even use that word, which she really couldn't—wasn't going anywhere.

Anna righted herself, taking a step away, and Colin dropped his arm. She busied herself petting Millie, who lapped up all the attention as if it was her due, going so far as to sprawl on the floor, belly up, waiting for Anna to rub her tummy.

Colin slid past Anna into the kitchen, turning on the lights so she got a glimpse of a comfortable if rather messy space with a low ceiling, a bright red Aga, and an oak table covered with papers and dirty dishes. When she trusted herself not to look or seem embarrassed by their near-clinch in the doorway, she turned from petting Millie and went into the kitchen.

"Your kitchen is on par with your car."

"Actually, I tidied today. A little." With a sheepish smile Colin whisked a dirty plate and cup from the island and dumped them in the deep farmhouse sink.

Anna came further into the room, her gaze moving from the sink full of dirty dishes to the far wall that was only half-plastered.

"This looks like a work in the progress," she remarked.

"Um, yeah." Colin rubbed the back of his neck, his sheepish grin still in place. "Has been for a while, actually."

"You mentioned something about five years..." The more time she spent in the kitchen, the more she noticed the unfinished touches. One wall was blue, another one had splotches of green against dirty white. Half a dozen two by fours were stacked against the half-plastered wall and looked as if they had been there for some time.

"Sorry, this really wasn't a good idea, was it?" Colin said with a grimace. "I'm afraid the whole house is like this. I was going to do it up slowly."

"Was?"

"I don't have a lot of time," Colin admitted. "And truth-fully, I always want everything to be perfect and so I end up doing nothing rather than something less than. I gutted the whole place originally. An old guy lived here, hadn't updated it since the 1940s."

"It will be beautiful when it's done," Anna said diplo-matically, because it was obvious that was not going to be any time soon.

Colin smiled wryly. "Thank you for saying that. But the spare room is clean—mostly—and the sheets definitely are."

"So you said. And I'm glad you're reaffirming that."

"I'll show you." Anna followed him up a narrow, enclosed staircase, dodging the tottering piles of books and papers on several of the steps, to the upstairs hall landing, also crammed with bookshelves overflowing with tattered paperbacks.

"Here we are." He gestured to a room that, in comparison with the rest of the house, was as clean as Colin had promised.

An old-fashioned wrought iron bed and a gorgeous oak armoire took up almost the whole room. A single window looked down on a tangled garden, the bare branches of various trees and bushes glittering with frost under the moonlight.

"Sorry," Colin said, "it's a bit crowded in here."

"It's lovely." She turned to him with a smile that she felt right down to her toes. "Thank you for everything. You've been so generous and kind."

"It's been no problem. I've enjoyed it. Getting to know you, I mean."

"Me, too." They grinned foolishly at each other for a few moments before it turned awkward and they both looked away.

"Right, then." Colin slapped his thighs. "Cup of tea before bed?"

"That's such a British thing," Anna said with a laugh. "But why not?"

"I'll put the kettle on." He disappeared downstairs and Anna sat down on the bed with a creak and a sigh.

Her heart felt as if it were flip-flopping in her chest. This was all so strange, and yet also kind of wonderful. Which made it dangerous, because nothing was actually going to happen. Was it? Why was there, even now, a question mark in her mind?

She took her pajamas and cosmetic bag out of her suitcase and laid them on the bed and, with nothing else to do, she tidied her hair, took a deep breath, and headed downstairs.

Colin had made an endearingly pathetic attempt to tidy the kitchen in the few minutes she'd been gone, pushing papers into random piles and hiding dirty dishes with a dishtowel. The kettle was boiling merrily on top of the Aga and, after clearing it of a newspaper and a single leather work glove, Anna sat down on a stool by the island.

"I expect you're one of those maniacally neat people?" Colin said as he poured their tea.

"No, not really." Mark had been rather fastidious, although he hadn't done much housework himself. He'd just hired an expensive cleaner. "A bit neater than this, though." She propped her chin in her hand as she watched Colin move about the kitchen.

"You know, I haven't even asked what you do. For work, I mean."

"I'm a freelance editor. I worked at a publishing house but I quit about three months ago." When she hadn't been coping, and her bosses had started to notice. She'd opted out before she'd been fired.

"And the freelancing is working out?"

"Yes, it gives me a lot of freedom." Which so far she'd used mainly to stay in bed with the covers drawn up over her head. But she had a few clients and after New Year's she'd make sure to get a few more. Get going with life.

Colin handed her a thick mug of sweet, milky tea and then took a sip from his own. "And what did your fiancé do?"

The question was unexpected. "Mark? He's in finance. Stockbroker."

"Now that surprises me."

"Does it?"

"I pictured you with an intellectual, artistic kind of guy. Someone who goes to art galleries and plays the guitar."

Not him, then. She took a sip of tea to hide the expression on her face, which she feared was disappointment.

"Nope, although I dated a guy like that in college. Those types can be a little high maintenance." She smiled. "But Mark... when I first met him, he was a lot more relaxed and laidback than he became later. The city rubs off on you, I suppose, gives you a hard shine."

"Did it rub off on you?"

"A bit. But I guess I always imagined leaving it eventually. Same as you." She tried for a smile. "I had it all pictured perfectly in my head. The minivan, the dog, the farmhouse in Connecticut, the family. Then it turned out Mark didn't want any of those things."

"I'm sorry."

"Well, like with you, better to find out before we said the vows than after, right? I should have realized before he asked me to marry him." Which had been something from a movie—the nice restaurant, the champagne, the ring from Tiffany's.

Meanly perhaps, Anna had felt like it had been too perfect, almost staged, as if Mark had watched an eHow video on how to propose.

"I guess those conversations are always a bit awkward. You don't want to seem like you're ticking things off a checklist."

"But whether or not you want children is kind of a big one."

"It's easy to make assumptions that someone wants the same things you do." He shrugged philosophically. "That's what I did."

"With Laura?"

He nodded. "Looking back I should have seen the signs. She bought me this shirt for Christmas, this expensive, tailored job from Savile Row. I wore it once and felt like a prat."

She smiled, imagining Colin in a fancy shirt, looking like he'd been straitjacketed.

"Those things seem small when they happen. It's only later you gain some perspective."

"Have you gained some perspective?"

"I'm in process. I realize I sort of sleepwalked through my relationship with Mark. He was attractive, wealthy, funny, charming… that seemed like enough."

Colin raised an eyebrow. "But it wasn't?"

"Not in the end. I'm grateful in a way we broke it off when we did."

They sipped their tea in silence, the only sound the persistent, hopeful thump of Millie's tail against the weathered wooden floorboards.

"So, Christmas Eve tomorrow," Colin said when he'd finished his tea and put it in the sink, along with all of the other dirty dishes.

"You must have plans."

"No, actually, I don't. I'm meant to go to Emma's for Christmas as usual but frankly I wouldn't mind missing the whole thing."

"Not on my account." Anna protested. "Honestly. I've gatecrashed your life enough."

"Seriously, I wouldn't mind." He held her gaze for a moment longer and a thrill rippled through her. Was he implying he'd rather spend Christmas with her?

"Somehow, having encountered your sisters for all of ten minutes, I think they would, a lot. And I don't want to come between a man and his family."

"How about we compromise, then? We spend Christmas morning together and then we both endure my family's prying and enjoy Emma's roast dinner in the afternoon."

The way he spoke, it almost sounded as if they were a couple, negotiating a lifetime of shared Christmases. And, God help her, she could almost imagine it. She could picture herself rolling her eyes at Colin as Emma fussed over him and he accepted it good-naturedly. She could picture lazing about on Christmas morning, sharing private presents—and a lot more.

She felt as if she already knew the in-jokes, the habits of Colin that would both annoy her and endear him to her. She could see herself in this kitchen as if it were her own, or setting up a study in the spare bedroom. They'd have to move the big armoire...

Good grief, why was she thinking like this? If Colin could see into her mind, he'd be horrified. It was scary, really, like falling down a rabbit hole, how quickly she could see herself slotting into his life.

And anyway, what about *her* life? Her family, her friends, her studio apartment on Avenue B, her Saturday mornings at the corner café with an almond croissant and a double espresso, her lazy afternoons at the Angelika Cinema, watching indie films with friends? She'd miss all that. She knew she would.

And it wasn't as if she even had a choice, for heaven's sake. She had to keep reminding herself she barely knew Colin. All right, they'd had some intense conversations and they definitely shared some chemistry, but it wasn't as if—

"What is it?" Startled, Anna jerked her unfocused gaze back to Colin. He was smiling faintly, yet with a frown settling between his eyebrows. "You looked as if your mind was going a mile a minute."

"I suppose it was." She shook her head ruefully. "Sorry. Just thinking about Christmas."

"Maybe it's time for bed." His tone was practical but Anna's mind went there anyway. *Bad Anna.* Colin plucked the empty mug from between her fingers and dumped it in the sink. "The washing can wait till morning."

"Why do I think you say that a lot?"

He laughed, a deep chuckle that had Anna smiling back. "Come on, Millie. Time for bed." Millie scrambled off the floor and Colin threw the dog a knowing look. "You're ready for your bedtime biscuit."

Anna hovered by the stairs while Colin took Millie out and then settled her in her dog bed before giving her the much-anticipated biscuit and turning off the lights.

"Ready?" he asked Anna, and she nodded, struck again by how intimate and yet normal this all seemed.

They headed upstairs together, the wooden floorboards creaking under their combined steps, and then on the hall landing they paused, the intimacy of the moment like a warm blanket draped over them, drawing them together in a snug cocoon. Through a half-open door Anna could see Colin's bedroom, a king-sized bed with a rumpled, navy duvet and a lot of clothes scattered on the floor.

"Goodnight, Anna." Colin's voice was a low murmur, a tendril of sound that snaked inside her and wrapped itself around her heart.

The smile she gave him was tremulous and hopeful, expectant. "Goodnight."

Another moment, a heartbeat of waiting... it would be so easy, so *right,* for him to take a step closer and brush his lips across hers. Anna was practically on her tiptoes, ready for it, already anticipating the feel of his mouth on hers, but then Colin smiled and took a step backwards instead, towards his bedroom. Was that regret she saw flashing in his eyes? Or had she just been horribly obvious?

With another murmured goodnight, Colin turned towards his bedroom, and so Anna had no choice but to retreat into hers. She closed the door behind her and in that moment the soft click felt like the sound of disappointment.

Chapter Seven

ANNA WOKE TO the smell of frying bacon. She lay in bed, blinking up at the ceiling, her mind a tumult of half-remembered, rather erotic dreams in which Colin had had a starring role. Why hadn't he kissed her last night? For a second she'd thought he'd at least been thinking about it, unless she'd read the situation entirely wrong. The possibility she had was enough to make her close her eyes, cringing.

Well, there was nothing she could it about it now. Slipping out of bed, Anna yanked on a fleece and a pair of jeans, ran a comb through her hair and brushed her teeth before heading downstairs.

The kitchen looked transformed. Anna pretended to stumble back in shock, one hand clutching her chest. "Am I in the same house?"

"All right, all right," Colin called good-naturedly.

He was dressed in a faded, gray t-shirt and even more faded jeans, and both pieces of clothing showed his powerful frame to perfection. Anna had the urge to run a hand along his stomach to see if his abs were as taut and sculpted as they looked.

"I figured I ought to clean up, considering."

"Considering?"

"I have a houseguest."

"Where did you put all the stuff?" she asked as she perched on a stool. The island and table were both completely clear, their wooden surfaces freshly scrubbed.

"In my study upstairs. Don't open that door on pain of death."

"I consider myself warned."

"Coffee?"

"Yes, please. Can I help?"

"Nope." He handed her a ceramic mug of coffee and Anna wrapped her hands around it as she watched Colin fry bacon and eggs. She felt rather remarkably happy. "I haven't asked you if you like bacon and eggs," he remarked as he slid two fried eggs onto a plate. "There's toast if you don't."

"I love bacon and eggs." She assured him. "Makes a change from the usual bowl of cereal standing at the sink."

"I thought we could go for a walk today, if you wanted?" Colin said when they were both seated with their fry-ups. "I know you've seen a bit of the village, but there's a nice stroll along the Lea if you're interested."

"That sounds lovely," Anna answered hesitantly. "But I feel as if I'm commandeering your entire holiday…"

"I don't mind." Colin looked down at his plate as he toyed with a forkful of egg. "I'm enjoying it."

Her heart flip-flopped just as it had last night. It felt as if Colin had made a bigger admission than perhaps he'd meant. Or maybe that was just more of her wishful thinking.

"So am I," Anna said, and they shared a quick smile, complicit before they finished their breakfast.

After breakfast they did the washing up together, developing a bit of banter over greasy plates and soap suds, and then Anna went to get dressed for their walk, meeting Colin a few minutes later at the front door with Millie frisking around their heels.

It was a glorious day, cold and brisk, the stark branches of trees thrust up against a pale blue sky and wintry sunlight making everything glitter.

Colin led her through his garden, a wild tangle of bushes with one half-finished raised flowerbed, a stack of two by fours propped up next to it, damp and starting to rot.

"The garden is a work in progress as well?" She surmised and he grimaced in acknowledgement.

He was a funny sort of perfectionist, Anna mused as they turned down a narrow footpath that ran along the Lea River, which at this point was little more than a burbling creek with steep sides covered in now-bare blackberry brambles. With his messy house and careless ways, Colin didn't seem like a perfectionist, not the way Mark had been, so fussy and fastidious, running a finger along furniture for dust, pursing his lips in disapproval all too often. But perhaps Colin wasn't actually a perfectionist. Perhaps what really happened with his projects was that he simply lost interest. The thought was almost enough to steal the glow from the day, until Colin pointed out a couple of ducks swimming in the river, and Millie began to bark madly. Anna decided to stop overanalyzing everything and let this one day speak for itself.

They walked along the river for half an hour, through what was in spring, Colin told her, a lovely bluebell wood, and then over a quaint wooden footbridge and across a tufty meadow tipped with frost before they came out at the top of the village, by the primary school.

"You know, I always thought the Cotswolds were quite tony," Anna remarked as they walked past some very normal-looking terraced houses. "You know, all electric gates and designer shops and organic farms."

"Well, there's plenty of that." Colin acknowledged with a bit of a grimace. "But there's plenty of locals as well, who were here long before the Londoners decided to swan out here and turn everything in to their *Country Life* fantasy of rural living."

"But you're not bitter or anything, are you?" Anna teased.

"How can I be, when they all want kitchen extensions?" Colin answered with a grin. "They keep me in business, those snobby Londoners."

"So really you should be thanking them."

"I suppose I should."

They walked across the school playing field to the top of

the high street, and Anna breathed in the cold, clear air, pausing to enjoy the view of the narrow street with its terraced shops sloping down to meadows of varying shades of green that stretched on to the blue horizon.

"Tomorrow's Christmas." She mused as she caught sight of the lights strung along the street lamps.

"So you've said. Are you regretting being on your own for Christmas?"

"I'm not on my own." She shot him a quick smile, and his look of pleased gratification sent warmth stealing through her.

"True, but the whole mum and dad bit. The stockings, the presents…?"

"Wait, I'm not getting presents?"

He laughed then, and so did she, something loosening and lightening inside her.

"I like hearing you laugh." They'd stopped at the top of the high street, before the shops and houses began, meadow on one side and the playing field on the other. It felt as if the whole world was holding its breath.

"I like laughing," Anna admitted.

"It seems as if you hadn't done much of it recently," Colin said quietly and after a second's startled pause Anna nodded.

"Life's been kind of hard, as you can imagine." She gazed out at the street, the tumbledown buildings of golden stone, the crooked sign on the pub, the charming yet authentic quaintness of it all. She couldn't look at Colin, not when she felt stripped bare emotionally. "For the first time I can see ahead to a point when perhaps it won't be quite so hard, and that feels amazing."

"I'm glad." His voice was low and heartfelt and even though it was dangerous she turned to look at him anyway.

Her heart stumbled and tripped at the intent look in Colin's eyes, the soft smile on his face. Affection and desire together, so heartfelt and sincere, there was no denying it this time. No denying anything.

Anna moved first, but Colin met her halfway, their mouths bumping together with clumsy gentleness, the cold press of their lips sparking something inside Anna's soul. She grabbed a fistful of his coat to anchor herself and her mouth opened and that awkward first brush of the lips suddenly turned into something far more insistent... and far more dangerous.

Colin slid his hands down to her hips and pulled her towards him. He was a man who knew what he was doing. A man who was as strong and capable in this as he was in everything else. She tilted her head back and they kept kissing; she forgot to breathe. She felt as if she didn't *need* to breathe; all she needed was this. Him. Kissing her, forever.

A car sped by, and the sound of it had them breaking apart, both of them looking startled and vaguely guilty. *Now what?*

"I..." Anna began, and then found she couldn't finish.

Her lips were buzzing.

"Let's walk," Colin said.

Grateful for the distraction, she nodded and they started down the street. She barely took in the shops decked out in festive wreaths and lights, the sound of bells jingling as doors opened and closed. Her mind was spinning, spinning, wondering how she was going to navigate this new level of—what?

If they'd stopped the kiss at that first sweet press, they could have explained it away. A little lapse, a temporary slip, the spirit of the holiday, blah, blah, blah. But, no. Anna had grabbed him, opened her mouth, made it into more. And there was no explaining away that blissful moment of hungry, unabashed passion. Just remembering it made her blush, squirm, and smile all at once. She didn't dare even look at Colin.

At the village green, she stopped and glanced at the impressive Norman church on the opposite side with its squat, square tower.

"What about going to the carol service this evening?" she asked.

"Sure. The one near midnight is candlelit, has a nice feel. Quieter."

Which was clearly code for no kids. She imagined the noisy, happy press of children at the five o'clock family service and shot Colin a quick, grateful smile without meeting his eyes. "That sounds good."

For some reason as they started walking back to Colin's house, a gray, glum feeling settled over her like a fog. It was *Christmas*. And while she'd thought she'd wanted to get away from it all, she found now that she was missing the festive spirit a little bit. Not the presents, precisely, but the trappings… decorations, Christmas carols, eggnog, and shortbread. That happy, bubbly feeling that only holidays could promise.

"So you don't decorate for Christmas, I gather?" she asked Colin as they stepped into the hallway.

He glanced back at her, shrugging off his beaten-up waxed jacket. "How can you tell?" His easy smile faltered as he took in her undoubtedly glum expression. "What's wrong?"

"Nothing." Anna felt silly for being down about it.

She'd chosen this, after all, and Colin had already given more of his company and consideration than she'd any right to ask for or expect. And that kiss had been the present she could have asked for. And yet she still felt like something was missing. She wanted a little bit of the real Christmas spirit. "I suppose I'm just missing all the Christmas stuff a bit. Like a tree."

"A tree?" Colin raised his eyebrows. "We can manage a tree."

Hope lit up like a candle inside her, emerged in a shy smile. "We can?"

"Sure. I can cut down a tree in the garden and plonk it in

a bucket of dirt. I've even got a box of ornaments down in the cellar, but they're all the naff ones my sisters didn't want."

Anna wrinkled her nose at the word. "Naff?"

"You know, the pinecones covered in glitter that I made when I was six. The crocheted Santa Claus Emma made in art class. Talk about looking like a crazed serial killer."

Anna laughed. "Those are the kinds of ornaments I love." The kind she'd never have, because she wouldn't ever have the children to make them. But this time, instead of letting that thought settle on her like a cloud, she pushed it away, choosing the sunshine. "Then why don't we have a tree?"

"All right, then." Within minutes they'd trooped out into the back garden, which stretched farther than Anna had realized, across the river, and into a small wood. He found a spruce that was big enough to be a decent tree without overtaking the room and started to saw. A short while later the tree was in the sitting room, which was as unfinished as the rest of the house, although Anna could imagine how it might look done up, with its big stone fireplace and the beams running along the ceiling. Right now it held a huge, battered, and overstuffed sofa, a scuffed coffee table, and, surprisingly, a piano.

"Do you play?" Anna asked and Colin shook his head.

"No, I've always wanted to learn but I never got around to it. My dad played, though. He could hear a song and play it, anything, just like that. My mum was going to get rid of the piano when she moved to Portugal and I offered to take it." He glanced at the dusty instrument, a faraway look in his eyes. "One day I'll learn."

"Yes," Anna agreed. "You will."

Colin went down to the cellar to retrieve the promised box of ornaments, and before too long Anna was helping him unpack them, laughing until her sides ached at the scary look on the Santa's face, just as Colin had promised.

While she was putting the finishing touches on the tree Colin warmed up some soup, and they ate with their bowls on their laps in front of the fire he'd built, admiring their beautiful if rather makeshift tree.

The gloom Anna had been feeling had dissipated entirely, and a new contentment had taken its place.

"This is a much better Christmas than I ever envisioned having," she said after they'd finished their lunch.

"Me too, actually." The ensuing lull in the conversation suddenly felt tense, expectant. Anna gazed into the fire, pretending to be mesmerized by the flames, even as her body started to tingle and she wondered if Colin was going to say anything—

"We haven't talked about that kiss." His voice was low, sure, and yet with a question in it.

Anna took a deep breath. "No," she agreed. "We haven't."

"Do you want to talk about it now?"

"Umm… well…"

"I'll take that as a no."

She thought she heard a smile in his voice, and felt a mingled rush of relief and disappointment. Colin rose to take their soup bowls, and Anna watched him go, wondering if she'd wanted to talk about that kiss after all.

Chapter Eight

THE NIGHT WAS starry and crisp as Colin and Anna walked through to the village to the midnight carol service. They'd spent a pleasant afternoon pottering about the house; Colin had tidied and done some work while Anna had read and then had asked, shyly, if she could make shortbread. Amazingly he'd had the ingredients on hand and something big and bright had bloomed in his chest when he'd sat at the kitchen table getting on top of his paperwork and Anna had bustled about, measuring flour and sugar.

Admittedly it wasn't the way most people spent their Christmas Eve, but the normalcy of it made Colin want it even more. He wanted days laughing with Anna, doing normal stuff, whether it was walking or cooking or playing Scrabble in front of the fire. He didn't care if it made them seem like an old, boring couple before they're time, he wanted it. He wanted her. She felt right here, in his life, in his arms.

Was it crazy to be thinking this way? It had to be, con-sidering they'd only spent forty-eight hours together. Every person he knew would tell him he was stark raving mad for contemplating a future with a near-stranger. But his gut, and maybe even his heart, told him he was right.

Although he had no idea if Anna agreed. She certainly hadn't wanted to talk about the kiss—the kiss that had just about blown him away, with the unexpected passion that had burst like a fireball between them. Colin had nearly embarrassed himself in the high street of all places, going for an even more explosive clinch.

He hadn't even meant to kiss her; at least, he hadn't been planning on doing it right at that moment. He'd certainly been thinking about it a lot, though, and hoping it might happen.

Perhaps that passionate kiss had been a natural progression of everything that had happened between them these last few days, the emotional intimacy as well as the chemistry, the sheer intensity of spending all this time together, and so suddenly and unexpectedly. But did that mean it wasn't real? What made something real or not, anyway? It hurt his head to second-guess himself as well as Anna and wonder what was going on. If he felt this way, why couldn't this be real?

Of course there was the rather major detail of Anna living on another continent. Hell, he was spinning some future for them when Anna was walking out of his life in about ten days. That was an obstacle he didn't particularly like to contemplate.

"You're awfully quiet." She glanced at him sideways, a smile lurking in her eyes along with some uncertainty.

"Just thinking." On impulse he reached for her hand.

He felt the surprise ripple through her but she didn't pull away. Her slender fingers twined with his and Colin's heart expanded like a balloon in his chest.

And balloons could pop.

He'd had that happen before, right in his face. Laura had pulled off her engagement ring and dropped it like a pebble into his palm, and he'd had no idea it was coming. She'd shaken her head, resigned and despairing, that he'd been so clueless. *Don't you see how much we want different things, Colin? But you wouldn't, would you? You never see anything. You aren't going anywhere. Everything in your life is a work in progress that is never going to be finished.*

Harsh words and he'd absorbed them, accepted the truth. Yes, his house was a mess. And yes, maybe he had a little issue with finishing things—but not *people*. Not what he'd considered the most important relationship in his life.

"Colin?" Anna's soft voice brought him out of his unhappy reverie. "Are you okay?"

"Yes." He squeezed her hand.

He wasn't going to think about Laura. She belonged in his past; he'd made peace a long time ago with the choices they'd made. No, right now he was going to live in this wonderful moment, with this lovely woman by his side. "I'm fine. I'm more than fine."

The church loomed ahead of them, the bells pealing

merrily, the sound carrying on the still, night air. Anna paused on the steps to look around; the village green glittered with frost and the houses across its verdant expanse were lit up cheerily, lights gleaming from their windows. The Christmas tree in the middle was aglow, a large, lopsided star shining on top.

"It's so lovely here," she said wistfully. Her fingers tightened on his. "So quaint and yet real, too. It's not…"

"Twee?"

She laughed, wrinkling her nose. "Twee? What does that mean?"

"A cross between quaint and naff, I suppose."

"I'm still trying to figure out what naff means."

"Those Christmas ornaments didn't enlighten you?"

"I love those Christmas ornaments. Especially the serial killer Santa."

Colin tugged gently on her hand and then led her into the church. The soaring ceiling danced with shadows from the candles placed on the end of every pew, most of them full. Colin headed for a mostly-empty pew in the back, and Anna slid in next to him, her thigh brushing his.

The service started; the familiar ritual of hymns and readings as soothing as the tidal pull of an ocean, an ancient lullaby. Colin leaned his head back against the pew and let the words wash over him as a feeling of contentment flooded his senses. He had the deep and innate feeling that this was where he belonged—in the village he'd never wanted to leave, with a woman who had only just arrived. It was crazy and nonsensical and yet somehow intrinsically right. He couldn't shake the feeling, and he didn't want to. He glanced sideways at Anna and catching his look, she smiled. He smiled back and squeezed her hand.

SOMETIME DURING THE day Anna had decided to quit second-guessing Colin's feelings—or her own. It felt a little bit like being caught in a riptide, thrilling and unnerving, especially as she realized she wasn't in control. But she was going with it, or trying to, letting each moment speak for itself, allowing the emotional current to carry her forward. She had no idea what, if anything, would happen when they got back home.

Home. The word had popped into her head unexpectedly and yet naturally. *Colin's* home. And yet for this brief time, hers, too.

After the service they stayed for the mulled wine and mince pies that seemed a prerequisite of any festive gathering in England. Colin chatted to a few people, his manner natural and relaxed, introducing Anna easily as a friend who was staying, simple as that. Anna caught a few speculative looks, the odd raised eyebrow, but it was all friendly. No doubt everyone was wondering who she was to Colin—just as she was.

They stepped out of the church at nearly one in the

morning, the moon high above, bathing everything in lambent silver.

Colin turned to Anna, a soft look in his eyes. "Happy Christmas."

"Happy Christmas," Anna returned. "I kind of like that better than 'Merry Christmas'." They stood there a moment longer, smiling at each other.

She felt Colin might kiss her again, there was that sudden tautening in the air, the curling of her toes, but they were standing on the church steps with people streaming by and so, after a brief pause where they'd just looked goofily at each other, she moved away a little and then started down the steps.

They walked in silence back to his house, and with each step Anna couldn't tell if she was gearing up or winding down. She felt nervous, that was for sure. They'd spent the whole day together but they hadn't talked about *that kiss*. She'd chosen not to talk about it, but now she wondered if she should have pressed the issue, especially since now she was contemplating so much more.

Millie greeted them at the door, butting their legs anxiously as Colin shed his coat. "Easy, girl," he murmured.

"She wants her biscuit?" Anna surmised.

"You guessed it. She's scolding me for being so late." He stood behind her as he helped her off with her coat and Anna was very conscious of his hands on his shoulders, and then sliding slowly, deliberately down her arms.

He hadn't turned on the light and every sense felt heightened in the darkness, from the touch of his hands to the sound of his breathing and the scent of his aftershave. A shudder went through her, impossible to suppress, and Colin stilled, his hands on her arms.

"Anna…" There was a world of longing in his voice, and it almost made her shudder again.

She stood still, silent, poised on this precipice, teetering, *teetering…* Gently, so gently, Colin pressed a kiss to the curve of her neck, his lips warm on her skin. The second shudder she'd been holding back escaped her in an audible rush. She tilted her head, unable to keep herself from doing it, to give him greater access to the sensitive skin.

Colin's hands tightened on her arms and he kissed her again, this time behind her ear. How could such a big, powerful man give such soft and yet earth-shattering kisses? Anna's knees nearly buckled.

With one hand, he brushed her hair to the side so he could kiss the nape of her neck. His body pressed against her back and Anna lowered her head, closing her eyes. Her resistance was melting like the morning frost but still she felt unsure. Or perhaps not unsure… just scared. Scared of what might happen, what it might mean.

Colin moved back a little. "Anna?" Her name was a question—one she didn't know how to answer.

"We never did talk about that kiss." Her voice came out in a hoarse whisper.

Colin tightened his hands on her arms for a second, his breath sending a shiver across her skin. "Let's talk about it now."

"I don't know what to say."

He stayed there for one aching moment, and then he dropped his hands and moved into the kitchen, tripping over Millie and nearly sending himself flying before he righted himself by grabbing onto the kitchen counter.

"Now that was smooth." He turned to her with a wry smile. "Definitely added to the moment. Very classy."

A bubble of laughter escaped her, lightening everything inside her. "Actually, I think that was perfectly timed. Comic relief."

"Was needed?" He cocked his head, looking at her as if he was trying to see right inside her. "Seriously, though." His gaze was soft and sincere and very blue. "What are you thinking?"

"Well…" Anna took a deep breath. "A lot of things."

"Such as?"

"That I don't do flings. Or one-night stands." She blurted the words and then felt herself blush. "I never have."

"Me neither. Well"—he raked a hand through his hair, giving her a sheepish, guilty smile—"there might have been a few in uni, I confess. But since then…"

"So what is this?" She gestured to the space between them. "Or should I not even ask that question?"

Colin pursed his lips, forehead wrinkled in thought.

"No, you should definitely ask that question. And I'll answer it, at least as best as I can. I don't what this is." He gestured between them just as she had. "But I'd like to find out."

"How?"

His grin was rueful and somehow sexy. "I could suggest the obvious…"

"Beyond the obvious," she answered with a laugh. "As tempting as that is right now, I admit."

"Glad to hear it."

"I live in New York City, Colin." She spoke matter-of-factly although her heart was beating hard. "You live in England. That seems like a barrier to the no-fling idea, straight off."

"A hurdle, perhaps."

"A freaking huge hurdle. I mean, if we're actually talking about having a relationship…" She shook her head, embarrassed by how much she'd said. "I mean, that is what we're talking about, right?" Maybe she'd got it all wrong. Maybe he'd just meant… some other kind of thing.

"Yes, that is what we're talking about. What I'm talking about. I don't know, Anna." Colin spread his hands. "I don't know how any of this could work. I don't know what the future holds. What I do know is that I've enjoyed the last forty-eight hours with you more than anything I can remember."

"But this is an extraordinary situation," she felt compelled to point out. "It might all change when we both have to go back to reality—"

"But this is my reality." He gestured to the kitchen. "I know it's not yours, and that's obviously an issue, but I'm not on holiday here. I'm living my life and you fell into it like—like the best Christmas present I ever could have had. As sappy as that sounds."

"It's not sappy." She felt almost near tears. "I..." Time to plunge. "I feel the same way. Being here with you has been... amazing."

"I feel like there's a 'but' in there," Colin said quietly. "You're not falling into my arms right now, so something's still bothering you."

"It's just... this has all happened so quickly. And the truth is we barely know each other." Even if she felt like she knew him, and that he knew her. A person couldn't really get to know someone in a matter of days, could they? A handful of hours?

Colin cocked his head. "Are you sure about that, Anna?"

"What do you mean?"

"I think I know you pretty well."

She stared at him, taken back and also intrigued. "How...?"

"Well, let's see." He raised one hand and began to tick off his fingers. "I know you're an only child with parents who dote on you. It's lovely, but also a little bit intense. They're always worried and so when life threw you for a loop you felt the need to back off, but you're missing them a little bit now, and even all the fuss they make."

"Wow." She swallowed. "That's scarily accurate."

"You've only been in a couple of relationships, and they were serious. The last one went on for a while. You thought it was going somewhere, but you lost sight of who you were along the way and you didn't even realize it until things started to go wrong."

She blinked. "Okay, what are you, a clairvoyant?"

"No, and I'm not even particularly emotionally intuitive, at least according to my sisters. But something about you speaks to something in me, Anna. I don't know why or how. It's just... I *get* you. Even though I know you're different from me, and your life is different, and... well, everything. You make sense."

It was the strangest and most heartfelt compliment she'd ever received, and it made everything inside her melt and yearn. "You make sense to me, too." The words were a whisper.

"You've broken up a big relationship and you found out life isn't going to happen the way you expected. So right now you're scared that you're jumping into something because of all the upheaval in your life and you can't trust it or yourself." He shrugged. "Only you can decide if you can."

"I know," she said.

She was stunned by how much he'd understood. How much he *got.*

"So I suppose I don't know you if you're talking about

what your favorite color is or where you went to primary school. I don't know if you had a dog growing up or what his name was. I don't know many of your preferences or dislikes, but that's the stuff you find out along the way, isn't it? And I'd like to find out." Colin took a breath and met her gaze directly. "But I think the question you really need to ask yourself is if *you* know *me.*"

Did she? "I know you're kind," she began slowly. "And that family is important, even if you act like they irritate you. I know you miss your dad more than you could ever say and you miss your mom, too, but in a different way."

"Okay," Colin said after a pause.

He sounded surprised and a little wary. Maybe she got him, too.

"I know you think you're a simple kind of guy, but you're not really. You're far more sensitive than you give yourself credit for, even though you might not like me saying it."

He gave a little self-deprecating grimace. "Probably not."

"I suppose the most important thing is that I know you're trustworthy. I can trust you." As she said the words she knew bone-deep that they were true. "But I don't know if I can trust me." She met his gaze with a direct one of her own. "It's been a hard few months, Colin, as you know. I'm only just starting to feel sure of myself again, getting a glimpse of who I was, who I can be. Embarking on a new relationship, especially one that has already got some pretty big challenges…" She shook her head, incredibly torn. "I don't know. I need to think about it, I guess. And I can't just… fall into bed with you. I'm not like that. I never have been."

"I'm not asking for that," Colin answered. "Hoping, maybe." He gave her a grin, although she saw disappointment and even sadness in his eyes. "But that's okay. We have all week, don't we?" He searched her face. "Will you stay here with me, while you're in England? Just to see? No expectations, no funny stuff, just time together…"

"Yes." That, at least, was an easy decision to make.

Colin's smile was like a wave breaking on the shore. "Good. Then we've got somewhere."

"Yes. I guess we have."

They gazed at each other for another few seconds before Millie whined, breaking the moment. "She needs to go to bed," Colin said. "And so do we." His eyes widened. "Separately, I mean."

She laughed, liking him more for the stumbling clarification. "I know."

"May I kiss you goodnight?"

The question sounded boyish, but when Anna nodded and Colin took in her arms, the kiss was not. His lips were sure and firm and really rather wonderful on hers. Colin was a man who knew how to kiss. Who kissed her like he loved doing it, and could do it forever. His kiss stole her breath and her heart, left her spinning. Colin released her, grinning as if he knew how affected she was. From the color on his cheeks, he was just as affected.

She playfully hit his shoulder. "You don't have to look quite so smug."

"Yes, actually, I do." Colin whistled for Millie. "I definitely do."

A short while later, as she lay in bed, she relived every glorious second of that kiss. The feel of Colin's strong arms around her, comforting and exciting at the same time. The sure press of his mouth on hers, the feel of her body cradled against his strength, as if he was sheltering her…

Why had she decided falling into bed with him was a bad idea? She was trying to be sensible. Cautious. But in that moment Anna wondered if she was just acting scared. Colin had already given her so much, and was offering her even more. Why not go for it and enjoy this crazy ride, see where it led? Jump in heart-first and let it all happen?

Her heart began to thunder in her chest as she considered what she was about to do. What she *wanted* to do. Then, before she could chicken out or second-guess herself, she threw off the covers and tiptoed out of her room. She stood in front of Colin's bedroom; it was silent inside. Was he asleep? Would she shock him? Did she even care? Taking a deep breath, Anna pushed open the door and stepped inside.

Chapter Nine

WHEN THE DOOR of his bedroom opened, Colin thought it must be Millie, hoping for another biscuit before bed. Sometimes, if he didn't shut the kitchen door properly, she snuck upstairs to beg. He really didn't expect it to be Anna.

Yet there she stood, at the foot of his bed, the moonlight streaming from the window lighting her hair and showing the uncertainty on her face. Colin sat up, his heart racing, his mind a little befuddled.

"Anna...? Is everything all right?"

"Yes." She let out a trembling sort of laugh. "Everything's fine. I just thought I'd... reconsider your offer."

Colin had once told himself he wouldn't make a play for Anna unless she came to him, naked and swaying, an open invitation in her eyes. And now here she was. For a second he thought of double-checking she was sure, ticking all those boxes, and then he decided against it. He'd been emotionally sensitive enough for one day, surely. And he wanted Anna. Badly.

He pulled the duvet off and opened his arms. "Then come here, woman."

Laughing, she fell onto the bed and then scooted across to him. The minute she hit his arms Colin hauled her against him, snuggling them both under the duvet, fitting their bodies together. The feel of all her softness against him was enough practically to make his eyes roll back in his head. Colin fit her even more closely against him, legs twining, hips bumping, her breasts pressed against his chest. Perfect, except he wanted more.

His mouth found hers and he couldn't keep from pulling back a little and looking down into her face. Needing to make sure she was sure, even now. So maybe he was that emotionally sensitive after all.

"What made you change your mind?"

Anna gave a small smile. "I realized I was being kind of ridiculous."

"Oh. Good." He kissed her again, deeper this time, his hands roving over her body, learning the feel of her, the roundness of her breasts, the dip of her waist and curve of her hip. She felt right. Everything about this, Colin decided as his mind retreated into nothing but sensation, felt totally and absolutely right.

ANNA WOKE TO wintry sunlight streaming through the curtains and her body feeling as if it were filled with molten wax. She felt lazy and sleepy and achy in a good way, in a lot of places. A smile curved her mouth as she relived a pleasant montage of the best moments from last night. The hard press of Colin's powerful body against hers, making her feel so small and precious. The exquisite pleasure of his touch and the way he'd moved, knowing what she wanted practically before she did, laughing against her skin as her responses slipped out of control.

The only tiny blip on the screen running through her mind was the moment Colin had asked about birth control, and Anna had reminded him, trying to sound light, that she didn't need any. A stumbling few seconds of apologies and clarification followed, and then Colin had picked up the rhythm and Anna's body's overwhelming responses had taken over and it had all been good. It had been wonderful.

But already she was wondering, *now what?* She twisted sideways to look at Colin, who was still asleep. Golden stubble glinted on his jaw and his lashes feathered against his cheeks. His face looked softer and more boyish in sleep, his hair mussed, his features relaxed. From downstairs she heard Millie whine and a glance at the clock told her it was after eight, and, she suspected, way past Millie's feeding time.

Carefully she eased away from Colin's loose embrace, grabbed the well-worn, navy blue, fleece bathrobe on the back of the door, and headed downstairs.

She let Millie out and then fed her a cupful of kibble before filling the kettle and plonking it on top of the Aga.

There was something strangely and intensely satisfying about simply standing there, the Aga letting out a comforting, rolling warmth as she waited for the kettle to boil and watched a few sparrows light on the stark branches of a tree outside. It was Christmas, and at this moment there was no place she'd rather be. She could, in fact, imagine being there for a lot longer.

The kettle clicked off and she made coffee, taking her mug to the faded, squashy armchair by the window. The sense of peaceful solitude lasted a few minutes longer before the old doubts and worries crept in, as Anna knew they would. They always did.

It wasn't just the geographical hurdle she and Colin would have jump that scared her now, but the emotional ones—namely the stark fact staring them both in the face that she could never provide Colin with the kids-in-the-back-of-the-Rover dream he'd shared with her. Had he even thought about that yet? Somehow she suspected he probably hadn't.

It was too soon to be tackling these huge issues with someone she was only just starting to know, and yet Anna didn't know what else she could do. They'd gone about their relationship the wrong way round, upping the ante before either of them had even realized they were in the game. And she'd compounded that by sleeping him with last night. She didn't regret it, but it made everything even more intense. And, to top it all off, she was going to his family's for

Christmas dinner.

What happened to starting things simple with a normal first date, movie and dinner and maybe a kiss? With a little groan she leaned her head back against the seat and closed her eyes.

"That wasn't a good sound."

Anna opened her eyes to see Colin standing in the kitchen doorway, a bemused look on his face. He wore a pair of flannel pajama bottoms and a worn t-shirt and, with his hair sticking up in about six directions, he managed to look adorable and sexy at the same time.

"Sorry. Just thinking."

"Hmm." He helped himself to a cup of coffee and Anna told herself to drop it. The last thing they needed was to battle through all the thorny things on Christmas morning.

"Nothing that can't wait," she told him lightly. "Tell me what I have to look forward to at your sister's."

"A very good roast dinner, a Christmas pudding from Marks and Spencer's, and a lot of nosy questions."

"What kind of nosy questions?"

"Well, they'll start out subtly," Colin said, bracing his hip against the counter as he took a sip of coffee. "Or at least they'll think they're being subtle. They'll ask you what you do and why you came to England and how you met me. Then, after the brandy comes out, the questions will become pointed and then, at least from Jane, downright rude."

"Wow." Anna took a sip of coffee. "Thanks for the heads

up."

"We don't have to go," Colin said seriously. "In fact, now that I think about it, I'd rather just stay here. Or preferably upstairs, in my bed."

"Not the spare bed?" Anna teased.

"We can go there, too. Any bed is fine by me. In fact…" He looked around the kitchen in an assessing manner. "This room works, too."

Anna laughed and shook her head. "You're…"

His eyes took on a wicked glint. "Incorrigible?"

"Yes. Definitely." She sighed and shook her head. "Seriously, though, I think your sisters would never forgive me if I stole you away from them twice in one week."

"They'd get over it eventually. Maybe." He shrugged, unrepentant. "Anyway, who cares what they think?"

"I should, don't you think?" The slightest of edges to Anna's voice had them both falling silent, staring at each other uneasily.

How many conversations like this would they jump into, left with no choice even though it felt too soon? How much emotional muck to wade through when they didn't know each other well enough to anticipate how deep it would be, how much they would flounder?

In that moment, Anna knew there were lots of way she didn't get Colin. She didn't know how he responded in arguments, if he'd be annoyed or patient or just try to ignore the tension. She didn't know how big a deal a stony silence or a sharp look was. She didn't know whether apologies came easily or were hard won.

"You know what?" Colin said, stretching out his hand. "Let's make this simple."

Anna looked at his hand, fingers stretched towards her. "How?"

"Let's go back to bed."

That definitely felt like the easier option, but it also felt like chickening out. Avoiding the fight. "But…"

"We don't have to be at Emma's till this afternoon," Colin said as he took hold of Anna's hand. "That's hours away." He tugged her gently up from the chair. "Bed."

And, smiling, deciding easier was better, at least for now, Anna went.

SIX HOURS LATER Colin stood on his sister's doorstep and tugged at the collar of the button-down shirt he rarely wore. He felt unaccountably nervous, prepared for the surreptitious—or not—grilling he was going to get from his family, but not sure if Anna was.

She'd been quiet this afternoon, after they'd emerged from their cocoon of covers in search of food. In bed, at least, there were no problems. He could happily relive, or preferably reenact, every moment of this morning again.

As for out of bed… what had seemed natural and right a short while ago now was starting to feel a little stilted and awkward. It wasn't Anna; he still loved being with her, was happy to while away an afternoon with her simply in the room, as well as a morning with the two of them in bed.

It was everything else—all the issues and unknowns that seemed to surround them on every side. Maybe toppling headlong into a serious relationship after forty-eight hours wasn't such a good idea. At least, it had some challenges that were starting to feel serious rather than simple obstacles he could swat away.

"Colin!" Emma opened the door, enveloping him in one of her split-second hugs before turning to Anna. "And Anna." Eyebrows rose for a fraction before her expression relaxed into a warm smile. "How lovely."

She hugged Anna too, and Anna returned it. Colin was glad Emma had opened the door. Jane would have been a different story.

They were propelled into the chaos of the kitchen—the twins running around, high on sugar and having too many new toys, and baby Will stuffed into a high chair looking overfed and dour. His sisters' husbands, Jack and James, shuffled over to make room for Colin, and while he'd like nothing better than to crack open a beer and retreat with the blokes, he didn't want to abandon Anna to his sister. Jane was definitely looking a bit beady.

"Anna," she said, her voice pitched between a bark and a trill, "so pleased you could come again."

The slight pause between 'come' and 'again' made Colin

inwardly wince. Anna's smile became a bit fixed. He never should have come here with her—thrown her in the deep end of his family, arms and legs flailing, not sure if she could sink or swim.

But if this is going to work, she has to handle it sometime.

Colin was fast realizing thoughts like that were not helpful, and especially not at times like this.

"Let me get you a drink," Jane said, shepherding Anna towards the girls' side of the kitchen by the stove, where Emma was mixing the Yorkshire pudding batter and Rose was stirring the gravy. "What would you like? Wine? Beer?"

"Um, a glass of wine would be lovely," Anna answered.

She threw Colin an uncertain look as he watched helplessly from the sidelines. Crossing over to rescue Anna would, he feared, be worse for both of them. It would show Jane that Anna couldn't handle whatever was coming her way, and that would undoubtedly make his sister pounce.

"So tell me again how you met Colin?" Jane asked and Colin closed his eyes and silently prayed for the day to be over.

SHE COULD DO this. She'd been telling herself so all afternoon and now she was going to choose to believe it. Anna took a sip of wine and gave Jane a steady smile. She would not let this pinched-mouthed academic intimidate her. She would not.

"Colin is my Good Samaritan," she said, her smile and

gaze remaining steady. "I was booked into your cousin Frances' B&B but it was flooded. He came to my rescue."

"Ri-ight," Jane said as if she was just recalling that. Anna was not fooled. "So you've known each other for…?"

"Three days."

Jane was, Anna decided, only just this side of bitchy. She got that Jane was his older sister, protective and all that, but there was a calculating glint in her eyes that Anna definitely didn't like. And so, because the flare of triumph in Jane's eyes was more than she could stand, she added, "but it's been an incredible, intense three days." She held Jane's startled look with a sweet smile as she saw Colin suppress a guffaw behind her. His delight in her comeback gave her courage. "As I'm sure you can probably imagine," she added with another sweet smile. "Or maybe you can't?"

Okay, that was bitchy and definitely not necessary. Anna took a sip of wine to keep from saying anything more. She was wired too tightly, but relaxation felt impossible when she was on the familial front line.

"Well, Colin has always had a thing for damsels in distress," Jane said, a steely glint in her eye.

Colin, no doubt now thinking Anna could hold her own, had retreated to the sitting room with the guys. Anna took a sip of wine to compose herself.

"Is that right?"

"You've heard about Laura?"

"Yes." But she had a feeling she was about to hear more.

"Now there was someone who needed rescuing." Jane glanced at her out of the corner of her eye to gauge her response. "A total mess, poor girl. She was in foster care, never had a decent family. Colin was always bringing her round, like she was some kind of stray."

Anna blinked, stung by the implication. She was the stray now, obviously.

"Colin kept trying to fix her just as he does with everything, but in the end he lost interest. Another unfinished project."

"*Jane.*" Rose glanced over at them, shaking her head. "Are you trying to put her off?"

"Just trying to be honest," Jane answered, all eye-batting innocence.

"Don't pay her any attention," Rose said with a frown for her older sister. "Jane likes to stir the pot. And she's always criticizing Colin—she thinks we spoil him."

"Well, you do," Jane said matter-of-factly. "And you can't deny it, Rose. Laura was a mess, and Colin got bored of her."

"I wouldn't say bored was the right word…"

Anna saw the uncertainty on Rose's face and felt a tremor of fear thrum through her chest. She could dismiss Jane's comments as plain nastiness, but Rose seemed genuinely nice. What was the real story with Laura?

"Well, anyway," she said, deciding to dismiss it all, "I'm here now."

Somehow she got through the evening. She stayed close to Colin for the rest of the night, and kept to chitchat. But the conversation with Jane remained like a bad taste in her mouth, souring her stomach. On the way back to Colin's she was quiet, and he noticed.

"So was that as bad as you thought, or worse?" he asked as they got into his Rover.

"I'm not sure," Anna answered honestly, and Colin turned to look at her.

"Seriously? Did someone say something to spook you? Jane, I'll bet."

"Well…" Anna wished she hadn't said anything.

She really didn't want to get into what Jane had said. She didn't feel ready to tackle that issue—and yet when would she? She was leaving here in a week. If she and Colin were going to try to continue and build on what they had, they needed to deal with this.

"What did she say?" Colin demanded. He sounded more forceful than she'd ever heard him, and it made her pause.

"What do you think she said?"

"Knowing Jane, just about anything." He hesitated, seeming to struggle with what to say next. "She's always resented me."

"Resented you?" Anna blinked in surprise. "For what, not finishing her kitchen?"

"What?" Colin looked confused. "No. She just gave me that kitchen job to punish me, anyway."

"*Punish* you?" Anna stared at him in astonishment, flummoxed by what Colin was saying. "What are you talking about?"

Colin's hands tensed on the steering wheel and then he let out a heavy sigh. "She blames me for my father's death."

"What?" She really hadn't expected that. "Why?"

"Because he was with me when he died. Because... because I was pushing him so we could finish the job on time." Colin looked out the window, his jaw working. "Hell, sometimes I blame myself."

"Oh, Colin." For a moment Anna couldn't speak. She'd had no idea he'd been dealing with this kind of guilt. There was so much she didn't know about him.

"So what did Jane say?" Colin's voice was leaden.

"It doesn't matter," Anna said, because now it didn't.

"You don't want to tell me?"

She tried to smile. "Are we having our first argument?"

"No. I was just wondering."

Anna took a deep breath. "She said you rescued Laura and then you got bored of her."

"Bored?" Hurt flashed in Colin's eyes, although whether it was from what Jane said or Anna repeating it she didn't know. "Laura was the one who broke up with me."

Anna shrugged. "I don't know the story, Colin, obviously. That's what she said."

"And you believe her?"

"No, but I don't know what to believe. We haven't

talked much about our former relationships."

Colin was silent for a long moment, his steely gaze on the road. "Look, Laura might have needed a bit of rescuing at the start, but it wasn't like that. She had a crap family and we started as friends in secondary school. I didn't get bored. I just didn't want to move to Burford or somewhere else tonier and live like some posh tosser. That's what Laura wanted, maybe because her background was so hard. But in the end she left me because I wasn't on board with it." He took a deep breath. "Satisfied?"

Clearly she'd touched a raw nerve. "I wasn't challenging you, Colin, and I wasn't asking to know any of that." Her voice took on an edge as she added, "You *asked* me what Jane said, and I told you."

"Sorry," Colin said after a moment, his voice abrupt.

They drove in silence the rest of the way back to his house. *Had* it been an argument, she wondered as Colin unlocked the door and Millie ran outside. The air felt thick and heavy with their silence. Was Colin angry, or was this normal? She didn't know, because she didn't know him well enough—and her ignorance felt more gaping, more insurmountable, than ever.

They went upstairs together, and Anna hesitated on the landing, because where did she go? This was still so new, so fragile. Maybe Colin wanted some space. Maybe—

Then Colin turned and reached for her, pulling her against him, burying his face in her hair. A shudder went through his body. Anna wrapped her arms around him and they stayed like that, unspeaking, a single unit, until he silently led her to his bedroom.

Sometimes a person knew instinctively what to do.

Chapter Ten

THEY HAD A week. A glorious week of lazy mornings in bed and afternoons walking or talking or simply spending time together. A week that felt both surreal and intensely real at the same time. A week that Anna never wanted to end. A week when they didn't, not even once, talk about the future.

Perhaps it was cowardly not to make plans, not to tackle all the roadblocks that made a relationship feel like an obstacle course only an emotional Olympian could navigate. Still, the issues were there, ever present, looming; they'd just gotten good at dodging them.

Perhaps it was wise to live in this oh-so pleasant stasis; Anna wasn't sure if either of them was ready for the kinds of conversations they needed to have one day, if they were going to make it work. But as the day of her departure loomed, she knew they had to talk about some of it. Either that or say goodbye forever.

"You could change your plane ticket." The words came out of Colin unexpectedly one evening two days before she was meant to leave. Anna had been stirring pasta sauce at the big Aga while Colin set the table for two.

She looked at him, startled, waiting for more.

"You're freelance, aren't you?" he continued, his gaze on the table in front of him. "You don't have anything to get back to."

Something about his tone rankled. "Just because I'm freelance doesn't mean I don't have *anything* to get back to."

"You know what I mean."

She pursed her lips. "I can't change my life just like that—"

"*Anna.*" He looked exasperated.

Maybe she was being prickly, but something about the way he approached the whole thing made her uneasy. Of course she was the one who would have to change. Move. She'd slot into his life, not his into hers.

"Fine, I could change my ticket," she agreed. "Give us a few more days, maybe a week. But what then? I have to go back home, Colin. Because New York *is* my home. I have an apartment, a job, friends, family. Plants that need watering." She was silent, waiting for him to say something more, but Colin just kept setting the table, his forehead furrowed.

"If we want this to work, one of us is going to have to give," he said at last.

Anna stared down at the bubbling red sauce. "And it's not you?"

"I didn't say that."

"I know. I inferred it." She sighed and stirred the sauce without enthusiasm. "Look, I get that if someone was to move eventually, it would most likely be me. Taking you out of this village would be like… like transplanting a camel to the Antarctic."

Colin looked up, bemused. "I'm not sure how I feel about that comparison."

"But it all feels too soon," Anna persisted, her voice catching. "I can't just give up my life after a couple of days with you. I wouldn't even be allowed to live here without a visa. I don't know anyone besides you and your family, and they're not all that crazy about me at the moment."

"I don't care about them."

"But you do." Anna insisted. "Family is important to you, even if they annoy you. Anyway, that's not even the point. The point is… I can't just stay here, without any sort of real life." Colin looked mulish and Anna persisted, trying to make him understand. "How would you feel if you arrived in New York with nothing to do?"

"I don't know," Colin said, a hint of sullenness in his tone. "But in any case I'm not expecting you to completely uproot yourself immediately. But the long distance thing can only last for so long."

Anna stared down at the sauce, a pressure building in her chest. Colin was right but she knew the geographical issue was only part of the problem.

"Anna?" he prompted gently. "I'm not trying to be

pushy, but I know we need to figure something out. There are ways around this."

"Are there?" She took a deep breath and then plunged ahead even though she didn't want to. "What about children, Colin?"

"Children?" He sounded startled by the leap in conversation.

"Yes, your whole dream of the kids and dog in the back of your Rover. I can't give you that. I never will be able to." She risked a look up to see him frowning at her.

"We don't need to think about that now—"

"But we do"—she cut across him—"I know it feels like I'm jumping the gun way too much, but if we're going to attempt this thing with all the difficulties it already possesses, you need to make sure it's what you want. That I'm what you want. And I can't ever give you your own children." Tears pricked her eyes and she blinked them away impatiently.

She'd known this conversation would be hard, whenever it had happened, but she hadn't realized quite how hard. Stating the truth so plainly still hurt. Perhaps it always would.

"What... what kind of infertility do you..." Colin asked after a moment, his words trailing away. "I mean, are there treatments? How is it that you're not..."

"I was diagnosed with advanced premature menopause four months ago." She spoke flatly, almost coldly.

She hated that he'd asked. She knew where his mind was going, down the blind, dead-end alleys of IVF, surrogacy, yada, yada, yada. None of it could work for her.

Colin looked confused. "I... I don't know what that is."

"Basically my ovaries gave up the ghost. No more eggs, no more periods, no fertility. By the time I was diagnosed it was too late to freeze eggs or save anything. I had a hysterectomy, it was the easiest way. I'm on HRT for the health benefits but basically... I can't have kids, not with IVF, not with a surrogate—at least not my own genetic child. *You* could, with a surrogate."

Colin grimaced. "Let's not go there right now."

"Well." She hunched her shoulders. "All I'm saying is, it's not possible for me. Ever."

"I know. I get it." His voice was quiet, his tone giving nothing away. The ensuing silence felt awful. "Of course," he continued after an endless moment. "You—we—could always adopt. If it—we—came to that."

It was way, way too early for this conversation, but what choice did they have? "That's true." She sighed, the conversation feeling like a leaden weight that had settled in her stomach. "That's what people always say. You tell them you're infertile and their expressions cloud for a few seconds and then they perk up as if they've just discovered the cure to cancer and say 'oh, but you can adopt'. And it *is* true," she continued, her voice turning a little ragged, "I can adopt. *We* could adopt, if we ever got that far. And adoption is great, it's awesome, I know it is, but... the reality is, for me, it would be a second choice, it would only because I couldn't have children of my own." She risked a glance at his expressionless face. "And I think it would be for you too."

Another endless silence. "That doesn't mean it would be bad."

"No," Anna agreed, the words dragged from her slowly. "But it's still a second choice. Something less than." Which was how *she* felt, how she'd felt since she'd been given the diagnosis.

Colin let out a ragged breath and scrubbed his hands over his face. "This is too much to process right now. We've only..."

"Known each other a week?" Anna filled in with a humorless laugh. "I know. Everything feels rushed because the truth is neither of us is getting any younger and if this is it... or if it isn't it..."

The words hung in the air, neither of them finishing that sentence. The silence stretched on, punctuated by the bubbling of the sauce on the stove, a mundane yet happy sound at odds with the tension and unhappiness Anna felt in the air, in herself.

"Maybe... maybe we should wait and see," Colin said slowly.

A new, creeping sense of dread stole into her stomach. "Wait and see?" she repeated numbly.

Colin didn't look at her as he explained. "Wait a month.

And then see… how we feel."

She stared at him, trying to hide how hurt she felt, how *horrified,* by that suggestion. He lifted his head to smile wearily at her, and she saw the lines of resignation in his face and realized, with a ripple of icy shock, that he was going to let her go. And she knew then that she'd been waiting for him to fight for her, for *them*—to battle all her doubts, slaying them like dragons.

But he wasn't, she acknowledged hollowly as Colin looked away again. Just as she was, he was seeing all the difficulties, the challenges, the impossibilities. And he was telling her to wait and see.

She knew how that would go. They'd wait a month, maybe send a few brief texts or emails in the meantime, although even those would peter out. Maybe they'd have an awful Skype call where both of them would talk at the same time and then laugh uncomfortably to fill the awkward silences, feeling nothing but a sorrowful relief when the call ended. They might try again, or talk about scheduling a visit, but the halfhearted plans would come to nothing and six months from now they'd be nothing but a shadowy memory in each other's lives, something to bring a smile touched with sadness to their faces. That was what *wait and see* meant. That was what Colin was suggesting.

And so Anna gave the only answer she could, considering the circumstances. "Okay," she said.

THAT NIGHT COLIN held Anna in his arms and wondered where he'd gone wrong, and how badly. Their conversation in the kitchen had felt like a breakup but he hadn't meant it that way. At least he didn't think he had. But Anna had been coming at him with so many difficulties, and he didn't know how to solve them all. He'd started, in a terrible, treacherous moment, to wonder if he ever would. *Or should.*

Everything had happened so suddenly, and Anna had expected him to process huge life decisions in the space of a few seconds. And when he hadn't, she'd looked at him as if he'd failed her.

He still didn't see why she couldn't stay a little bit longer, let them figure this out together. Tackle things a bit more slowly. But Anna had made it clear she had a life in New York to go back to, a life, it seemed, that wasn't going to include him. And he didn't know if he could change that.

Anna let out a soft sigh, her eyelids fluttering, and he stroked her hair. This felt like goodbye, but he didn't want it to be. He wanted things to be simple, but maybe they couldn't be. Maybe they just weren't. The infertility thing had thrown him for a loop; he supposed he hadn't given it too much thought until that moment, hadn't realized quite how final it all was. And, he'd realized, after knowing someone for a week—one *incredible* week—it didn't feel fair or right to have to make the decision that he'd be okay not having kids, ever.

Sighing, he closed his eyes. He didn't know how to fix

this. Part of him wanted to wake Anna up and reassure her he didn't care about any of the stuff she'd thrown at him, but that didn't feel right or truthful. He couldn't just sweep everything under the rug or pretend it didn't matter. It did matter. He just wasn't sure how much, or what the future held.

For the first time in a week, he wondered if he and Anna had one.

THE LAST DAY in Wychwood-on-Lea felt like a funeral. She and Colin did all their favorite, familiar things—if she could even use those words after a single week. Colin cooked a huge fry-up and then they took Millie on a long, rambling walk by the river, up through the meadows high above the village, and then down the high street.

Anna felt as if she was saying goodbye to everything, and each silent farewell tore at her heart. She didn't want it to be like this. She just didn't know how else it could be.

That afternoon it started to snow, big, soft white flakes that looked like something from a fairy story. Anna stood at the kitchen window and watched them drift down, covering the world in white.

"Your flight shouldn't be delayed," Colin said, his voice sounding unnaturally loud. "The forecast says the snow will taper off tomorrow."

They hadn't had a normal conversation all day; it had

been all stops and starts, throat clearings and awkward laughs. All of it made Anna sad.

"Oh. Okay." Anna paused. Was she supposed to be pleased? She didn't feel it. At all. In any case a couple of hours or even a day or two of delay wouldn't make a difference—would it? Anna felt like she didn't know anything anymore.

On her last night Colin insisted they go out to Wychwood-on-Lea's one bistro, and Anna agreed because it felt easier. When they were surrounded by people they wouldn't be able to have a painful heart-to-heart, which was a good thing. She couldn't bear Colin stumbling through some awful *it-was-fun-but*. She'd rather he said nothing at all.

In the end they chatted about nothing in particular, jobs and movies and, at one low point, the weather. Then, after the waitress had brought their after-dinner coffees, Colin put his hands flat on the table and said. "Anna."

She paused in stirring her coffee, her eyebrows raised as she waited for the speech she'd been hoping to avoid.

"What's going on here, really?" Colin asked. "I feel like we're breaking up but that's not necessarily what I want."

The *necessarily* felt like a stab wound. It was worse than a maybe. "What do you want?" she asked quietly.

"I don't know." Colin gazed at her, clearly frustrated. "I want things to be simple but I know they're not."

"Nothing's simple, Colin." Now that she knew him a bit better she understood how he operated.

He acted as if things were always simple because he wanted them to be. She'd been drawn to that clear sense of certainty at first, but now she saw that when things *weren't* simple, Colin backed off. Stopped trying. And she couldn't make someone try.

"Fine, some things are simpler than others."

"Let's make this simple, then," Anna said. She couldn't bear any more bumbling about the truth. "We haven't known each other long enough to decide whether we want to spend the rest of our lives together, or for one of us to make the huge commitment of moving continents for the sake of this barely-begun relationship. So let's just trust fate or providence or whatever you like that if we're meant to be together, we will be. Our paths will cross again, one day." She smiled as if to show this was a great plan.

Colin glared at her in disbelief. "Seriously? That's your plan?"

"You've got a better one?"

He stared at her for another moment and then slowly shook his head. Anna felt as if a crack had splintered down her heart.

"No," he said. "I guess I don't."

SO THAT WAS that. Everything seemed to speed up after their conversation. Colin paid for the meal and they walked out of the restaurant in silence, the world a blur behind the tears

Anna was trying to blink back.

That night Colin reached for her in bed, and they made love with a quiet passion that bordered on desperation, their bodies in perfect yet sorrowful sync. Afterwards, lying in bed, her body still thrumming, she had time to think—and she came to the unwelcome conclusion that she'd been another one of Colin's fix-it projects, left as unfinished as the half-plastered wall or the paint splotches. He'd cheered her up, shown her how to be happy again, and now he was leaving. Or rather, she was leaving… but he wasn't stopping her. And Anna couldn't even blame him.

The next morning she packed her bag and Colin insisted on driving her to the airport. She climbed in his battered old Rover and looked back at the village as they drove out; she could see the steep gabled roof of Willoughby Manor above the tree line, and had a pang of envy for the unknown people who would be moving into Willoughby Close and making their lives in this lovely village.

And then Wychwood-on-Lea disappeared around the bend, and half an hour later they were speeding down the motorway, and another hour after that they were at the airport and Colin was saying goodbye.

"Let's not make a big deal of this," Anna said in a rush. "I don't want to cry."

"But it is a big deal," Colin said. They hadn't spoken much in the car and now he looked both angry and miserable. "A very big deal."

"Thank you," Anna said, managing a trembling smile. "For everything. I mean it, Colin. I was at such a low point when I came to England, and you helped me to be happy again. For that I'll be forever grateful." Even if right now it felt as if her heart would be forever broken.

Colin's eyes looked suspiciously bright. "I wish it didn't have to end like this."

"I'm not sure there is another way."

He didn't protest, just drew her into his arms and rested his chin on her head. Anna closed her eyes, both savoring and hating the moment, knowing it would end all too soon and wishing that it didn't have to end at all.

Colin eased away first. "Ring me," he said. "Please. To say you arrived back safely."

Anna nodded, even though she knew she wouldn't. She'd email instead. A conversation would be too awkward and painful. Colin had given her a ream of contact details, and she'd duly given hers back. It felt like exchanging addresses at the end of summer camp, when you promised to write and then never did.

She stepped away. "The security line looks long. I should go."

"Okay."

She didn't say goodbye. He didn't kiss her. It was only later, when she was on the plane, when she let herself feel all the emptiness whistling through her and sorrow came for her like a howl in the dark, that she wished, quite desperately, that she had.

"YOU'VE BEEN A sorry old git these last few weeks, you know."

Colin looked up at his sister Jane, who stood in the doorway of his kitchen. It was seven o'clock in the evening and he was contemplating having cereal for dinner. And a beer. The usual, then, although actually he hadn't eaten much these last few weeks.

Now he eyed Jane grumpily. "What are you doing here?"

"Visiting you." Jane stepped into the kitchen and Mille came over to her with a hopeful sniff. "Emma rang and said she was worried about you. And I can see why. This kitchen is a tip and you look terrible."

"Worried about me?" Weetabix it was. Colin took down a box. "My kitchen is always a tip."

"Because you're avoiding people and the pub, and even the Rugby Club. So something is clearly up. Or perhaps down." Jane leaned against the counter, crossing her arms. "Is it the American?"

"The American's name is Anna, Jane."

"Fine. Anna. Is it her?"

"No. Yes." Colin rubbed a hand across his face.

He was bone-tired, mainly from working all hours be-cause the alternative was sitting around and moping. Remembering all the sweet and sexy moments he'd had with

Anna. All the tenderness, all the laughter, and yeah, all the sex. But not just that. Hell, he missed making dinner with her as much as anything else. He missed Anna, full stop.

"I miss her," he admitted, although why he was telling Jane he had no idea.

When their dad had died and their mother had move to Portugal, Jane had taken over as parentis in loco. The trouble was, Jane didn't have a maternal bone in her body, as far as Colin could tell, and certainly not one for him.

"She did say the week was intense," Jane said with a small smile. "I think she was trying to shock me."

"And you were trying to cow her."

"I was being protective."

"Or vindictive?" Colin said before he thought better of it. Spending too much time working alone had made him lose his social filter.

Jane looked properly surprised. "Vindictive? What do you mean?"

Colin sighed. "Forget it."

"No, I won't." Jane took a step closer to him. "Why do you think I would have been vindictive, Colin?" She looked curious but also troubled.

He didn't want to say it, didn't want to go there with Jane or anyone. Three weeks after Anna had left and he still felt steamrollered. Letting her walk away had felt like the only thing to do, but it hadn't felt right. Nothing had since then. He'd gone over and over his actions and words, and he didn't know what he could have done differently. What Anna had wanted him to do.

"Because of Dad," he said at last.

It had been fourteen years since their father had died so perhaps it was time they had this conversation, even if Colin still didn't feel like it.

"Dad?" Jane's eyebrows rose almost comically. "What do you mean?"

"You blame me for Dad's death," Colin said starkly. It felt weirdly good to say it out loud. "Because I was working him too hard. Or maybe because I went in with him on the business. Whatever. If it hadn't been for me, he could well still be alive." Jane was silent for so long Colin forced himself to look at her. "No denials?" Not that he expected any beyond the paltry.

"I don't blame you, Colin," Jane said quietly. "Maybe I did, for a moment or two, in the depth of my grief, I admit. When someone dies there's always a time of wondering how things could have gone differently, what I could have done…"

"Or what I could have done," Colin interjected. "Or not done."

"I don't blame you." Jane insisted. "If you think…" She took a deep breath, seeming, for the first time since Colin could remember, near tears. "If you think I'm being vindictive because of *that*… I admit, I can be prickly. And direct. But I'm not out to get you, for heaven's sake!" She brushed at her eyes. "Besides, Dad was so thrilled to be part of Heath & Son. He told me so. He told everyone. And he never would have let you push him. He'd have pushed himself." She sighed, the sound ragged. "I don't think he would have changed anything, even knowing how it would all turn it out. It was his dream, to go into business with you. If anything, I was jealous of that."

"Okay." Colin's voice was hoarse. "Well, cheers for that."

She nodded, and they both remained silent for a few minutes, sniffling and trying to act as if they weren't on the cusp of some major emotion.

"So," she finally said, slapping her hands down on the counter top. "What about Anna?"

The swerve in conversational tactics startled him. "What about her?"

"You and Dad took a risk in starting a business," Jane pointed out. "Why can't you take a risk with Anna?"

"It's not that simple."

"The distance?"

He grimaced. "Among other things."

"Have you talked since she left?"

His grimace deepened. "I've emailed." When the email back had been a terse two lines he'd felt both angry and hurt, and so he'd left it. Anna had, too. Stalemate, it seemed, again.

"Well, either she's important to you or she's not," Jane said. "That's simple, at least."

Colin couldn't believe his forty-four-year-old ever-single sister was giving him relationship advice.

"So what do you think I should do? Fly to New York and surprise her?"

He said it for her to scoff, but Jane merely raised her eyebrows. "Why not?"

ANNA STARED AT the same line of boring medical text that she was meant to proofread before slamming down the lid of her laptop and getting up to make a cup of tea. Her productivity had plummeted in the three weeks since she'd been back in New York City. Since leaving Colin, she hadn't been able to concentrate on anything, except perhaps her broken heart.

As much as she tried to talk herself into believing that particular organ was fine, she didn't buy it. She spent the nights lying in bed, reliving every one of Colin's caresses, and the days in a fog of misery, wishing he were there.

Her parents were worried about her, after she'd driven to Connecticut for a New Year's visit, and she'd done her best not to mope about and failed. Her friends were worried about her, because she kept refusing offers to go out and hid in her apartment instead. She was worried about herself.

When she'd seen that email from Colin, hope had flared hot and bright inside her, only to wink out when she read the stilted lines. *Hey Anna, hope you got back okay. Hope to hear from you, Colin.* He might as well have been emailing an acquaintance. And maybe that was how it had felt. After a few bittersweet days, he'd most likely been able to get right back into normal life. He'd have finished the cottages of Willoughby Close; the first tenants would have moved in. He'd get some new contracts, head to the pub or the Rugby Club, laugh about his holiday fling and then give a philosophical shrug. She could see it all and, heaven help her, it hurt. Meanwhile she was drifting around her apartment like a ghost, barely able to string two sentences together on her laptop.

A knock sounded on the door and with a sigh Anna went to answer it. It had to be one of her neighbors, since the front door of her building hadn't buzzed. Elderly Lois from upstairs asking if she'd gotten her mail—she hadn't—or traveling businessman Paul from across the hall, reminding her to feed his cat next week while he was away. The joys of city living.

She opened the door. Stared. Felt her jaw drop and still no words came. *Colin.*

"Surprise." His smile stretched and wobbled and Anna smiled back.

"You've definitely surprised me." He looked so good was her first thought.

The same bright blue eyes, the shock of light brown hair. The weathered face and powerful build, the sheer size and ease of him. She wanted to run into his arms but suddenly she felt shy. His coming here was a good thing—wasn't it? Still she didn't know what to say. To feel.

"May I come in?" Colin asked, and hurriedly she stepped aside.

"Yes, yes, of course. I'm just so…" She smiled, emotion burning like a bright ball in her chest. "Surprised."

"So, is this a good surprise or a not-so-good one?" Colin asked as he came in.

His voice cracked and she realized how nervous he had to be. How much he'd risked, coming here unannounced, hoping she'd be glad to see him.

And she hadn't risked anything.

In a sudden rush of realization, Anna knew how much she'd played it safe all along. She'd wanted Colin to do all the heavy lifting, shining knight to her damsel in distress, assuring her it would all be okay while she kept whining that it wouldn't. Why hadn't she tried harder? Fought harder? Been stronger?

She'd chosen the cowardly option every time. She could have delayed her flight. She could have scheduled a visit. She could have determined to give their relationship a real try, instead of backing off, hands held up, shaking her head sorrowfully.

She'd been a coward because she'd been scared. Scared that Colin would tire of her, that she wouldn't be enough for him, because that had been her fear all along.

And yet… he was here now. And maybe that was all that

needed to matter.

"I've missed you," Anna said, because those were the first words that came to mind, the first words that needed to be said, and the truest.

"Good. Because I've missed you like crazy." He cleared his throat and then spoke in a stumbling rush. "Look, I know it's going to be hard, and we still have a lot to work out, and there's the distance thing and the children thing and God even knows what else, but I've realized, Anna, that I want you in my life. A lot. And I hope you want me in your life, too." He let out a shaky breath and ran a hand through his hair. "I needed to get that out."

"I needed to hear it." Anna knotted her hands together, anxious even now. "I'm sorry, Colin. I chickened out back in Wychwood-on-Lea. I was afraid I wouldn't be enough for you. I'm still afraid. The children thing is big."

"It doesn't have to defeat us." Colin insisted. "It doesn't have to be everything, Anna. And it's okay to be afraid. I'm afraid too," Colin said, his voice rough with emotion. "Afraid of leaping into something this big, but even more afraid of losing it. Some things are worth the risk, Anna. You are."

She let out a funny little sound, something between a sob and a laugh, because he couldn't have said anything more perfect and, better yet, she believed him. "You are, too," she whispered. "Definitely."

She didn't know who moved first, but somehow she was

in his arms and he was hugging her so tight her feet nearly left the ground. And then he was kissing her, and her entire world righted itself. She could breathe at last. She could smile.

"I'm sorry I've been so scared about everything," she said when they came up for air.

"I'm sorry I let you walk away. I felt like we needed to figure everything all out and I didn't know how, but then my sister Jane talked some sense into me—"

Anna pulled back a little. "Wait, *Jane?*"

Colin grinned. "Yeah, Jane. Who knew, huh? I'll tell you more about that later. The main thing is she knocked some sense into me and I realized that maybe we didn't have to figure it all out now. Maybe all we have to figure out was that we need each other."

"I do need you." Anna promised him. "More than I even realized when I left."

"And I need you. I've been like an angry bear these last few weeks, growling at everybody."

The image made Anna laugh and she hugged him again. "So, is this our happily-ever-after?" she asked, her arms still wrapped around him.

"No," Colin said as he hauled her against him. "It's our happily-ever-beginning."

Anna snuggled against him. "I think I like the sound of that."

Epilogue

Six months later

"THANK YOU FOR choosing our airline and welcome to Heathrow Airport."

Anna stood up and reached for her carry-on, her heart as light as a balloon floating up to the sky. It was summer, the sky was blue with clouds like cotton wool, and she was about to step into Colin's arms. She didn't think it got better than this.

They'd spent the last six months pond-hopping back and forth, trying to see each other at least once a month. The trips had depleted their bank balances but filled their hearts, because with each visit, Anna fell more and more in love. In June, Colin had taken her to a charming hotel in Broadway, another beautiful village in the Cotswolds and a much nicer place than Frances' B&B, and asked if she'd consider moving to England. She didn't have to move in with him, just live in the same village preferably. Anna had agreed.

Less and less had tethered her to New York over the last few months. Friends got married, had babies, and moved away; her parents had expressed a desire to travel, maybe even rent a place for a few months in the Cotswolds. Her freelance work was going well and could be done anywhere. It was all falling into place so beautifully, like it was meant to be—because it was.

"Anna!" Colin waved from beyond the customs exit and, with a grin practically splitting her face, Anna headed towards him. She'd only seen him a couple of weeks ago but this felt different. Bigger, because she was staying. She'd decided not to move in with Colin right away, wanting to take it a little slow. She'd tried for one of the cottages in Willoughby Close but they were all rented. So Colin had found her a little flat on the high street, above the bakery. It smelled like sausage rolls but she didn't mind. She also suspected she wouldn't be there for too long.

As soon as she cleared customs, Colin started towards her, swinging her up into his arms and kissing her thoroughly. The dozen roses he'd brought fell to the ground, but Anna didn't care. She was just happy to have his arms around her and to begin the rest of her life.

"Good flight?" he asked when they both needed to take a breath.

"Great now it's over and I'm with you."

"Fantastic," Colin agreed and took her suitcase from her.

Anna slipped her hand into his, knowing she was in the right place, exactly where she wanted to be.

"Shall we?" Colin asked, and she nodded, her heart full

to brimming with happiness she'd never expected to have. "Yes, let's go home."

The End

The Willoughby Close series

Discover the lives and loves of the residents of Willoughby Close in the next book in the series out January 31!

The four occupants of Willoughby Close are utterly different and about to become best friends, each in search of her own happy ending as they navigate the treacherous waters of modern womanhood in the quirky yet beautiful village of Shipstow, nestled in the English Cotswolds…

Book 1: A Cotswold Christmas

Book 2: Ellie Matthews's story
Pre-order now!

Book 3: Ava Wentworth's story
Coming soon

Book 4: Hattie Lang's story
Coming soon

Book 5: Alice Owen's story
Coming soon

Available now at your favorite online retailer!

About the Author

After spending three years as a diehard New Yorker, **Kate Hewitt** now lives in the Lake District in England with her husband, their five children, and a Golden Retriever. She enjoys such novel things as long country walks and chatting with people in the street, and her children love the freedom of village life—although she often has to ring four or five people to figure out where they've gone off to.

She writes women's fiction as well as contemporary romance under the name Kate Hewitt, and whatever the genre she enjoys delivering a compelling and intensely emotional story.

You can find out more about Katharine on her website at kate-hewitt.com.

Thank you for reading

A Cotswold Christmas

If you enjoyed this book, you can find more from all our great authors at TulePublishing.com, or from your favorite online retailer.

TULE
PUBLISHING

Made in the USA
Monee, IL
28 November 2022

18870688R00095